# HEART

Part 1
Affairs of the Heart Series ~ London

## KEW TOWNSEND

Tremmelle Publishing

HOLLYWOOD, CALIFORNIA

© 2015 Tremmelle Publishing. United States
© 2015 Cover Design by Sparkle Graphics
© 2015 Cover images by Gianfranco Bella; By-Studio
© 2015 Book Cover Layout Jesse Kimmel-Freeman
© 2014 Interior Layout BookDesignTemplates.com

**Sign up for NEWSLETTER at www.kewtownsend.com**

**HEART/KEW TOWNSEND**
ISBN 978-0-6924427-0-8

# Dedication

To Jenna, the bravest woman I know.
My neverending love and admiration.
Before that.

# Acknowledgements

To the music, and the musicians from the 1950s to 1992 that inspired this story — the good old days.

Forever "thank you" to Jenna, who spent countless hours telling me "that's stupid" and I fixed it. A zillion thanks to my dedicated beta readers from long ago to present, you know who you are. To all the beautiful, lovely ladies that encouraged me with the magical phrase, "I want to be Holly!"

Hugs to you — the readers — that love romance and rock music. You motivate me to write the best story I can.

YOU ROCK!
KEW

kewtownsend.com

# CONTENTS

EIGHT MILES HIGH.................................................................1

LOVE IS STRONG ................................................................5

JUST ONE KISS.................................................................17

ONE OF THESE NIGHTS .......................................................23

BACKSTAGE PASS .............................................................33

LET IT RAIN.....................................................................39

ROCK YOU LIKE A HURRICANE............................................47

SMOOTH OPERATOR...........................................................55

LINGER .........................................................................67

CONSTANTLY CRAVING.......................................................73

SIMILAR FEATURES ...........................................................81

YOU'RE SO VAIN ..............................................................95

MAGIC MAN ...................................................................105

CRAZY FOR YOU..............................................................111

# Chapter One

# EIGHT MILES HIGH

## 1989

## London, England

# Day 1

Holly had a plan. The icy air conditioning in the first-class section of the airliner chilled her to the bone. Holly's hands shivered as she accepted the complimentary champagne to calm her frayed nerves. The jet sailed out over the deep blue Pacific Ocean, turned north to Greenland, and headed toward England.

Holly searched in her Louis Vuitton carry-on, for the Cable Music Television (CMT) business card with the London contact. *Where was it?* "Howard, that's right," she reminded with relief, straining to remember the rest of her instructions. Howard, the driver, would pick her up and a man named Hunter was all she recalled of the London CMT representative's name.

Her stomach stirred with a light excitement she wouldn't have expected as the plane started its descent. It pierced the pure white cloud cover to reveal spacious green hills, child-sized brick structures, then landed at Gatwick airport.

"England," she whispered.

Holly cleared customs with butterflies dancing in her stomach and searched for her name scrawled on a card. So many people met the plane with nameplates, but none spelled out Holly or Hill. She'd taken for granted the picked up would happen without problems.

"How could I do this?" she complained aloud, remembering this wasn't all a vacation. Holly sighed while wandering to the front of the terminal. A white Bentley touring car sat with a sign posting a familiar name, HOLLY HILL.

The tall, gray-haired chauffeur introduced himself as Howard and loaded her Louis Vuitton carry-on, and satchel into the trunk. As she stepped into the luxury car, a man caught her eye. Not a suspicious man, and not any man, this man looked like he'd walked off a Hollywood movie set. A tan Fedora hugged his head, securing long, straying, strands of silver-blond hair that blew wildly in the brisk breeze. The stranger's shoulders filled a well-worn, chocolate-brown bomber jacket. His long, lean legs were clad in tan Dockers, his feet covered in Rochnocs hiking boots and he carried a worn leather briefcase. As he bent his tall form to enter a classic olive-green Jaguar, he paused.

The moment froze in time.

She was delighted.

She'd captured his attention, as his purposeful stance pierced hers. His drop-dead, gorgeous face filled with an expression of surprise, but his eyes, hidden by reflective Ray Ban sunglasses, concealed his thoughts. A happy, elegant smile curled about his lips as if he unexpectedly recognized her.

A searing heat flushed her cheeks because she couldn't turn away. The handsome stranger pulled on the front brim of his hat to acknowledge her, bathing her in his generous smile. He bent gracefully and disappeared into the rear of the car.

"England," Holly whispered.

"New beginnings...."

# Chapter Two

# LOVE IS STRONG

Holly rubbed the back of her neck wondering if she should marry Brett Templeton. He'd proposed, and she'd accepted. She wondered if she could move forward with the engagement, set a date, and be sealed to a miserable fate with no chance of escape. Or, should she say no?

That question had pushed her to England. Hours ago, she would have thought not. Magically, the vision of a beautiful stranger in the airport provoked a new feeling — hope. More importantly, his radiant smile and attractive image had created explosive carnal stirrings she'd never felt for Brett.

The enchanting English sky was laced with fog like in the majority of fairy tales. A light breeze playfully danced in the trees as a greeting — her vacation in Jolly 'ld London was officially underway. No one could find her, not even Brett. A sweet peace washed over her because the plan, to get out of L.A., worked perfectly.

The strong scent of fish and chips stopped her at the

corner. She discovered a pub and went in to dine. She washed the tasty morsels down with dark ale as if an elixir to soothe her jet-lagged nerves. She decided it was time to venture out, explore London, because, in two hours she had to meet-up with Howard. She stepped onto the sidewalk. Her legs were wobbling from downing a large pint. She smoothed out her tawny, Donna Karan, silk mini-dress, with matching tailored jacket and threw her black Prada bag on her shoulder. The suit fabric was thin, and she shivered from the chill of the afternoon making her think about warmer clothes and a shopping spree. She covered her forehead to shade her eyes. A harsh flash of the blinding sun was suddenly set free from a cold blast of a frolicking breeze that danced around her whispering a sweet promise of freedom.

The toe of her gray Yves Saint Lauren heel barely touched the pavement of the street when she missed the curb, stumbled and fell. From nowhere a firm hand gripped her upper arm and jerked her to its owner. The sunlight spilled a brilliant golden backdrop. Evidently, she was standing in the presence of her guardian angel.

A British accent flowed from his lips as music.

"Carrin?"

So urgent was the familiarity of which he spoke the name, she wished she were Carrin.

"Forgive me. I meant Miss! You need to be careful," cautioned the charming voice, with a clear English accent.

Without warning, a concert of car horns spat angrily at her. The jolt of noise frightened her. She jumped forward, shoving her body into his, and her head crashed against his firm chest. One of his hands quickly braced the base of her head, holding her oh, so close.

The commanding male voice assured, "Don't be afraid," as he pressed his warm lips against her ear.

Holly welcomed his protective arms surrounding her waist, pulling her tightly against his warm, firm, slender physique. She leaned into his gentle hands that inched their way about her back exploring her like a familiar map. She grabbed his trim waist to balance. His voice was touching her again, a deliciously dreamy voice.

"You've been drinking?" he remarked, adding a tiny laugh — his tone of voice and words, merely an observation to explain her dangerous behavior.

Holly stammered, "I had English ale."

"Oh, you're American!" he confirmed as if laughing at her naivety, because of the strong potency of the brew.

The stranger held her closer, and she was his willing captive. His hard, invincible body molded to perfection into her curves. The rich scent of Italian leather accentuated his masculinity.

His hands came to rest firmly in the middle of her back.

"I see. No one has told you English beer is stronger?"

The blinding light forced Holly to turn her head away as she squinted to see him. "No, no one," she admitted, squirming to pull her hand free to shade her eyes, and get a clearer picture of this angel incarnate. While she took a step backward, the gentle English voice swamped her again, as his arms embraced her tighter preventing no escape. She leaned in as his chest expanded, taking in a deep breath as he lifted her. She was flying.

When her feet touched the ground, her forehead dropped

onto his fresh, scented chest, in the way of a long lost lover. Dark blond hair peeked out from his crisp, forest-green, cotton shirt. She caressed his chest with her cheek and relaxed against the length of him, nestling in closer because he felt good, safe, and right.

Holly lifted her chin, and her eyes filled with joy as she followed the long line of his smooth neck, inventing ways to press her lips against his inviting golden flesh and taste of him. It had been too long since a man felt this good — if ever. This man was perfect.

*For heaven sakes,* she chided herself. *Stop this foolishness. He might be married with ten kids!*

She didn't care as he moved in even closer. His fresh, clean scent trapped her, and a tiny groan vibrated inside his chest as his warm cheek nestled in her neck.

"Mmmm, you smell so good," he whispered.

Her mind clouded. *No man ever spoke to her this way.* The ways she dreamed a man did when his desires were aroused. He wasn't married, judging from the way this man held her — not this man. She glanced up as a cloud blocked the bright rays of the sun to reveal him. "It's … you," she stammered. Here he stood, tall, and shockingly handsome, the beautiful vision from the airport. She spoke in a low tone.

"It's you."

A puzzled expression narrowed his brow. "Forgive me, Miss. Are we acquainted?"

Holly bit her lip. Close to making an even bigger fool of herself, she would rather die than confess she'd fallen into instant, sinful lust at the sight of him. She squinted to focus in on his face. Oh, what a face, it was, with succulent lips, she longed to kiss.

The stranger lifted one dark, blond eyebrow above the top of his sunglasses.

She stifled a smile picturing his expression to be like a pensive English schoolmaster.

"Yes. I remember the airport." As icing on the cake, he added, "I wished you were in my arms, then. I never dreamed my wish would come true."

Surely, her cheeks must be red because she burned with embarrassment. No, she reassessed. She burned with red-hot desire as she sank deeper into the stranger's arms as if fingers into a custom fit glove. She stole a short, ragged breath, aware of the power and magnetism of this man. Another heated rush flushed her cheeks, and it stung.

"I need to get back to my hotel." *That was dumb.* It was not an invitation for him to go with her to the hotel room as it sounded — as *she wanted.* She added, "...to freshen up a little."

"If you don't mind a suggestion, a walk in the cool breeze might help to refresh you. And if I'm not intruding, may I walk with you?" He dropped his black Ray Ban sunglasses to perch on the edge of his nose.

There they were, dreamy blue eyes sparkling with delight and daring her to join him. Where was the strength to say no to his bright baby blues, which dared her 'join me in an adventure,' that might change her life? She wanted to explain she'd follow him anywhere. But she did not want to appear too eager and run off with a complete stranger.

Brett flashed in her mind. He was so blind to the fact that she would ever think of running away from him to England, so far away from his watchful eye. And he'd never believe she might become interested in another man.

No, this was a moment of reckoning. Would she go with him? Holly squeezed in a breath and eased back.

"Trust me," he coaxed, "I would consider it an honor to go with you." He hesitated. "Forgive me, a beautiful woman as you must be expected?"

Holly shook her head, letting him interpret there was no one.

His eyes brightened. "May I persuade you to come with me? Nothing compromising, on my English honor," he vowed with a glint of mischief in his eyes.

*Compromising. English honor.*

Holly looked straight into his flawless, suntanned face. His Fedora crowned his head perfectly. The hat and high collar of his jacket hid the exact length of his hair. Long, wispy locks blew freely about his chin. Her knees weakened at the sight of him. She hoped he was an English Rogue, and would abandon all decorum, and honor, and wildly ravish her.

Strangely confused by her conflicting emotions, she abruptly cooled, catching hold of herself and her lusty reaction to him. Even after seven lonely years with Brett, she wasn't desperate, well, perhaps deprived. Still, she'd never let on to him.

"No? Come, I'll walk you back to your hotel." He invited, dazzling her with a smile worthy of any billboard in Hollywood.

"Perhaps a walk would refresh me." She acknowledged, surrendering to those angel eyes that promised her a better time than she would ever imagine.

He wasn't moving and she stood locked in his embrace, her lips were inches from his.

*Mmmm. To savor those perfect lips, so ripe, designed for kissing over, and over again. So damn sexy.*

Her longing flared followed by a deep burn.

"Yes," she agreed, shook her head clear, and inhaled a breath of cool air. "Let's walk."

The handsome stranger pushed his sunglasses back into place with a brown leather-gloved finger. He stepped ahead of her a generous stride. Just the motion of his muscles moving under his tan Dockers ignited lusty feelings even deeper inside her. What was happening to her? She had never been so instantly attracted to a man.

He motioned to her to join him, saying, "Where in America do you call home?" A broad smile covered his face, revealing straight white teeth.

"California, Hollywood." She offered, postponing her examination of his body, moving quickly to catch up with him.

She came up alongside him, and when he smiled, he lit up the world.

"Smashing place, I've recently relocated there, a new job an' all."

That news put a grin on her lips. This man had prospects. The brown Pineider leather briefcase, he clutched, was the same model as Brett's that carried important briefs and Brett's cost thousands of dollars. Of course, Brett's was spotless. As a lead attorney at a respected law firm in Beverly Hills, he meant to impress. This stranger's briefcase was worn as if it had seen many business deals.

The handsome stranger interrupted, asking, "Are you in London on holiday?"

Too embarrassed to let on she was taking a break from her fiancé who was pressuring her to set a wedding date or the real reason, Holly highlighted her professional assignment. She hoped that would produce the least questions. "I'm here doing research, for a law firm I work at in Beverly Hills."

"Brilliant! Perhaps one day you can tell me where the fun places are in Beverly Hills?" he exclaimed with a promise of seeing her again.

Holly pushed a full, satisfying grin to her cheeks. Fantastic. This man likes adventure. It was about time things went her way. She laughed softly.

"I've said something to amuse you?" he asked and smiled for a moment before his beautiful face conveyed bewilderment.

Through the dark lens of his Ray Ban glasses, she saw his eyes cloud with confusion. "No!" She rushed to apologize. "I'm sorry. It's ... I work so much. I don't have any idea how to have fun. I wish I did."

He looked at her pensively for a second. A warm smile relaxed his sun-kissed face, he suggested, "Maybe we can remedy that. When I return, we'll find the fun places together?"

Holly noticed the mischief in his blue eyes hidden behind the black glass lens as they locked onto hers. He was making a future date with her, and she didn't know his name. She was transfixed, unable to take her eyes off him. Mesmerized by his impulsive proposal, Holly stumbled on a raised crack in the sidewalk, forcing her to break her fall by latching onto his forearm.

"Here, Miss? We've made plans for the future, and I don't know your name. Although after holding you, I have a sense I've always known you. What do your close friends at home call you?"

"Holly," she offered, regaining her footing.

"What a lovely name," he replied, and after a long pause.

"Here, take my hand to steady you."

She reached out to the well-mannered Englishman as he slipped his hand around hers. Once again, electricity passed from him to her. He was unbelievably reserved on the outside, but the energy flowing through his gloved hand was hot. What was she going to do with this handsome stranger? She tried to calm her shaking hand.

"Here, what's this? Everything's all," he reassured.

*Where have you been?*

Holly's Prince Charming guided her down enchanting, cobblestone streets, she never saw. They passed carts, brimming with the flowers in bloom, architecturally beautiful churches with magnificent stained-glass windows, and quaint boutiques, she wouldn't remember, because she was blinded by this man's chivalry and hopelessly lost in his enchanted spell.

During the comfortable silence, Holly briefly wondered what Brett would presume if he saw her now? Here she was walking hand-in-hand with a man who had devastating good looks. Nothing like Brett's GQ features because this man didn't have that contemptible self-confidence, better yet the conceit, Brett exuded around women. This man's gait was not one of arrogance. In fact, he seemed to avoid attention, but he must realize the disturbing effect he had on females. He walked reserved and perhaps too self-composed, for her immediate liking. He wore the culture of an Englishman judging how he had come to her rescue. Vivid, sensual images of him flashed in her imagination. Pictures of the two of them playfully rolling about on her bed, skin-pressing skin, locked in his hot embrace. The thoughts left her breathless. Struggling to regain any sense of decorum, she squeezed his hand. "I'll be fine after you tell me your name," she spoke with a quiet voice though she didn't care who he was. All that mattered was that he was here.

"I beg your pardon, Holly. Your beauty and charm have caused me to forget my manners. My name is Luka."

*Luka, so European.* It fits him perfectly, like everything else about him.

"Holly." She heard him say but hadn't answered. She already loved to listen to him pronounce her name with his ravishing British accent, his cadence, and pronunciation, so easy to understand.

"Holly?" Luka repeated. "Which hotel are you registered?"

"The Kensington Arms. Somewhere close to here. I'm confused."

"Yes, it's over two streets." He motioned, with his head, pushed his hat back off his forehead, and smiled. "What do you bloody well say I ring you later this evening? Take you to dinner?" His head remained half-cocked, and his lips wore a boyish grin. Nothing else about him was boyish — he was one hundred percent man.

That sounded perfect, what she hoped. But how safe was it? Her cheeks burned because of her inexperience with men, and he was a stranger. She responded, "I'm sorry. I have people to meet. I don't have my schedule, or what is planned until I check-in with them," she lamely offered.

Sensing her discomfort, he puts her at ease. "As do I, tonight I'm up against the same problem, pressing business. You are aware we will be jet-lagged and awake when all of London is asleep. Perhaps you would allow me to ring you when my business is finished. Give me a chance to change your mind?" Once again, his boyish grin shined in anticipation.

There was no use pretending she'd ever refuse Luka. But her hesitation caused his sunny smile to wane. Luka turned and pulled her closer to his chest. The disappointment in his eyes gave him away. He didn't want to leave her. It was working. He was fueling those vivid images in her head, the ones with her legs wrapped around him making, sweet love. The fiery strength of the swirling pictures scared her, forcing a flush of heat, causing a dizzy, eruption of feelings to ripple from head to toe.

"There's a pub that stays open late. Perhaps we might eat, talk, and I promise I'll take you back to your hotel straightaway before the jet lag kicks you in the back of your head."

Talk, she wanted more than talk. Holly took a bold step toward Luka, oh, so close. She hesitated, wanting to place her hands on his chest, wondering if she should, then did. "When do you think your business will end?" she asked as moisture laced the inside of her palms from the heat radiating from Luka's chest.

A slow smile curled at the corners of Luka's lips, understanding her intent and explained. "Well, I have time restraints. I'm free to call as early as midnight?"

"Midnight?" she said quickly, regretting she hadn't stopped herself from exposing her disappointment with the flat tone of her voice.

"Too early? Late?" He responded as his eyebrows rose to wrinkle his forehead.

"No ... it sounds like a fairy tale."

"Not quite," Luka reassured her. "Midnight was the end of the fairy tale. For us, that is the beginning..."

# Chapter Three

# JUST ONE KISS

**P**arked at the curb was the white Bentley. Howard stood waiting as promised. Holly stepped into the car — her coach. Her makeup was perfect. She'd secured her long, copper-cellophane-tinted hair, half-up, using a gold clip. She'd allowed the rest to flow down around her shoulders, falling to her waist over her garnet lace-trimmed camisole, that framed her plump breasts. She wore no jewelry, with a white, tailored, mini skirt suit by Anne Kline, gray heels and carried a black Prada bag.

"I love this royal treatment," she declared as Howard drove her past many brick cities to the outskirts of London. She thought back to the events leading to this whirlwind vacation. Yesterday, she had been quietly sitting at her desk at the law firm. Her confidential assistant, Lucy, had cautiously approached her wearing an oversized, plum knit top, over black leggings.

"Holly, I have to confess."

"Yes? You have my attention." She set the new case file

aside.

"You have been under an awful strain since the Collins murder trial ended. A few weeks ago, I followed an impulse, believing nothing would come of it, and that later we'd have a laugh. Still, I'm not sure you will like what has happened."

Holly sat back in her chair listening, wearing a puzzled expression on her face.

"I was at Tower Records on Sunset Blvd. and discovered a contest that CMT was sponsoring. For the first time in music history, they are underwriting the return of the super band *Hurrikaine,* and their new world tour *Lost Dreams ... Lost Illusions*."

"Interesting? I've heard of *Hurrikaine*. Everyone has, but I don't remember any of their songs. What does *Hurrikaine* have to do with me?"

Lucy hesitated before answering. "Well ... I filled out an entry ticket for each of my girlfriends, and I added one for ... you."

Exasperated by the story, Holly asked. "Again, what does any of that have to do with me?"

Lucy raised her eyebrows and announced. "There is no easy way to say this. YOU won!"

"WON?"

Lucy continued speaking very fast. "Yes, an all-expenses paid trip to London. Best of all, you are expected to leave in a few hours."

"Are you crazy? I'm not leaving with the new case starting and stacks of prep work ahead. Never mind that Brett wouldn't approve. What are you thinking?"

Lucy countered. "Yes, those are all valid arguments, but I

have it all figured out. First, the firm needs background work on the new client. I have convinced Brett to send you, and no, he knows nothing of the contest. Second, from what you've shared with me, Brett is pressuring you to announce a wedding date soon and where better to think than London. And three, forget about Brett and the contest business. That will take a few hours each day for promotions, but the concert will be fun and a drastic change from what's been going on around here. The rest of your day, go sightseeing. You have never been to London, and the weather is lovely this time of year. So thank me, go home, and pack, because your plane leaves in six hours."

"Why not?" Holly responded, surprising herself. She thought Lucy's argument was logical. Go on an adventure. Seven days away from Brett, seven days in London, the background investigation would take a few hours, and later a few hours with, oh, right *Hurrikaine*.

"Well, okay, but why do I leave tonight?"

"Some glitch in communication. CMT thought the materials were sent last week. When the packet information hadn't been faxed, they frantically called me because I'd listed my phone number on the entry form, but I haven't been home in days. CMT's booked a last minute flight. Everything is ready to go."

Lucy had made the impossible happen by creating down time to relax, have fun, and decide when she wanted to become Mrs. Brett Templeton. She'd been reluctant to set a date because they'd both recognized theirs would be a loveless union. And Holly thought a cuppa tea and biscuits sounded inviting.

Now, here she was in London, the adventure had started.

Wembley Stadium was like any arena, gigantic. Holly followed Howard as he created a pathway separating her from the thousands of *Hurrikaine* fans as he escorted her through the barriers protecting the concert personnel. Hundreds of backstage staff and road crew milled about and it was nothing short of a small city humming with excitement. Something important was about to happen here. *Hurrikaine* had arrived.

Howard took a step closer to her. "Miss Hill, I see Mr. Hunter."

"The CMT representative?"

"Oh, no, Miss Hill, he's CMT."

The walls of people everywhere blocked Holly's line of sight. The excitement and electric buzz charged Holly. Soon it would be time to start her contest obligations.

But what of Luka?

*Sweet Luka.* A warm, sinful flush filled her entire being.

"At the stroke of midnight," she whispered to herself aloud. Her plan? To linger in his tender embrace, until she was dizzy from his inexhaustible charms, and then rip his clothes from his body.

"Get a grip." Holly chided under her breath, how quickly she was changing under Luka's brief influence. Now, she had a Mr. Hunter to handle. She'd dealt with his kind before, a rich and powerful man. She had a business obligation to fulfill and then get the hell out of there.

"Come along, Miss Hill. I hope Mr. Hunter not angry and understands the traffic delays are why we've arrived late," Howard explained nervously.

The backstage chatter eclipsed many of his comments. Something great was about to happen, and everyone was in on it but her. Holly turned around in a circle. She was walking into something much bigger than she'd ever realized.

Howard politely placed his flattened palm on her lower back, guiding her along until he came up behind a tall man.

His blond hair was long, dripping below his shoulders and hung prettier than any California blond she'd seen along the coastline in her hometown of Santa Barbara. A black and brown leopard print scarf, tied like a halo about his forehead, held his golden hair in place. That was the last of him that reminded her of a pirate. A custom made, black-leather Concha coat hung to his knees. Below, torn, and frayed tipped Levi's that gripped well-worn Michael Anthony black leather boots.

Holly had to remind herself to stay put.

*Don't run away.*

She'd worked with many influential men like this one who was at the center and in control of this overwhelming production. She put a smile on her face to hide she was nervous because he was pure rock 'n' roll.

Holly took another step as if caught in quicksand. Howard urged her closer. She noticed the man's strong, British accent, bellowing above the wild bustle of the backstage activities, issuing orders like a general to anyone who passed. The man radiated power.

Swiftly, like a clap of lightning his hand dropped to his side. The crash of his brown leather glove, smacking against the leather coat, accented each piercing word he spoke.

"CMT's stupid, fucking, contest winner should be here straightaway! I don't want any bloody fuck ups. We have to meet the London curfew, and wrap this up early."

Holly's chin dropped to her chest. Here she stood — the stupid, fucking contest winner, realizing with the quickness of a lightning bolt that she was way out of her league.

*Run!*

Run back to her hotel, hide at the back of the bar, drown her crushed feelings in English ale, and wait for Luka to make her forget.

The brash, rude man, quickly turned around to greet Howard, who had gingerly placed his white-gloved hand on his shoulder.

Holly caught a ragged breath and slammed her eyes closed.

Too late to run, too late to hide.

# Chapter Four

# ONE OF THESE NIGHTS

olly stood her ground. She drew in a soul, strengthening breath and opened her eyes. Her jaw dropped slightly. She blinked rapidly and the rising blush stung her cheeks. The image before her did not change. Standing in the center of this bizarre crowd stood Luka. Her guardian angel was Luka Hunter, the CMT representative.

Momentarily taken aback, Holly shook her head until her hair covered her shoulders, yet her head was not clear. She wanted to run to him, or, should she run away from him? One thing was clear. One of her secrets was out. She was the stupid, fucking, contest winner, not an executive from Beverly Hills, sent to do research. She was here to see concerts, be photographed, and filmed with the elusive and infamous rock band *Hurrikaine*.

As the panic settled in her stomach with the punch of stampeding elephants, she remembered the bathroom basin so long ago. Would the image ever stop haunting her? Why was it whenever darkness trapped her, she pictured the razor's sharp edge and her oozing blood?

*No, no more.* "I won't run away this time. Luka's worth fighting my mountain of fear." She urged under her breath, making promises to steady her nerves. "I can do this, I must."

Holly fought back the clashing emotions, especially the humiliation that had followed to scorch her cheeks. The stupid, fucking, contest winner indeed! She wished to vanish from that exact spot. Holly raised her chin and called on all the years of experience she'd had hiding her reactions from the media, during, and after, each sensational, headline-grabbing criminal case.

She returned to her senses, realizing this was Luka standing in front of her, here, backstage, at the hub of a *Hurrikaine* concert. Her racing doubts slammed to a halt with lust a second behind because Luka was moving, taking another step closer to her. She lifted her gaze to watch his coat as it opened with each movement of his body.

*Mmmm,* his golden tanned chest draped with nothing but a black, silk vest. He was striking. Perhaps more stunning if possible, with his straight, golden hair glistening under the backstage lights. The different lengths framed his face cascading over his shoulders. But his hair was nothing compared to the sparkle in his cat-like blue eyes.

Astonishment blasted from his voice as he declared.

"You're the CMT contest winner?"

"You are Luka Hunter, the representative for Cable Music Television?"

He took a step closer, taking her hands in his as his eyes filled with joy and laughter. He released them to continue to inch around to the small of her back to hold her.

*You feel it too.*

She slid into Luka's arms with the comfort of a familiar lover and hugged him voraciously.

Luka pulled back, allowing a momentary chill to pass between them though he kept her locked safely in his arms. He threw a glance to Howard. "Remember to pick her up at the waiting area."

"I will Sir."

"Smashing." Luka's eyes sparkled, and narrowed.

"So, I didn't have to leave you this afternoon. Why didn't you bloody well tell me?"

Holly thought fast for an answer. She chose to tell the truth. "I was embarrassed. A well-meaning friend entered me in this contest, and I inadvertently won. Sounds ridiculous when so many faithful *Hurrikaine* fans would be honored to be in my place."

"I wouldn't have met you."

*She'd expect him to say that.* "For the record, *I am* here to do research for the firm." Damn, she had one confession left. She wondered if she'd ever tell him she was here to make a decision about Brett that would change her life forever. The admission shot a cold shiver through Holly.

"Are you all right?" He probed. "You're trembling."

She forced another half-lie. "It's so overwhelming to see you here backstage. I should have known you would be a man in charge."

Luka smiled. "I'm not important, a shadow, and I don't care how you came here. You're here now. That's all that bloody well matters. Me? I'm assigned to organize this circus. My misfortune, to work with the band the next two weeks until they finish their Paris, shows. It's cruel and unusual punishment because I have known them for years."

She arched an eyebrow. "Really, tell me about the *Hurrikaine.*"

"Spoiled sod," he ranted, stopped, and cleared his throat.

"Forgive me. I'm never in the presence of a lady, and it will take me a few moments to brush off my loutish manners." Luka raised his eyebrows, smiled, and spoke in a dignified tone. "I should have said — he can be extremely difficult when he wants to be." He followed with a boisterous laugh that floated like a breath of fresh air.

She was about to join in as her attention settled on a gathering of young girls standing on the side, groupies she'd assumed. They eyed her with suspicion and envy, followed by contempt. Especially when Luka released her only to slip his arm protectively around her waist as if to claim ownership. He drew her closer, close enough to dazzle her with his sizzling heat. In the meantime, he instructed three stagehands, with the precision of a conductor while his free hand dug into his pocket for his cellular phone. He took a call, pushed the antenna down inside, and dropped it back into his coat pocket.

"Stay close. The bands finally escaped the press tent. I assume this experience is new to you, and I am sorry to inform you, but you've signed on with the biggest concert event of the decade. You are the chosen one, the sacrificial lamb. Fate has picked you to witness *Hurrikaine's* triumphant return after a four-year hiatus."

Holly noticed the sarcasm lacing Luka's usually sweet

words. Why did he dislike *Hurrikaine* so?

"But luck is with you. Your late arrival means only minutes for a brief introduction tonight," he explained.

Luka paused, looking deep into her eyes.

He was too damn sexy, causing Holly to speak words she'd never expected. "I'm only interested in one thing."

He flashed a questioning glance.

She raised her brows with a developing confidence that surprised her. "Midnight."

Luka fixed his gaze on Holly as he complimented her in a sexy voice, "Have I told you how lovely you look tonight?"

"No, I would have remembered that. I must add you're very handsome yourself, Mr. Hunter." She offered, returning the compliment, pleased with her choice of wardrobe as she stroked the tips of his long shiny hair with a red manicured nail.

Luka wasted no time and moved in close, oh, so close. His leather-clad hand circled her waist swiftly and tightly pulled her into him once more. He spoke privately into her hair. "Midnight."

His moist breath blew on her cheek with a promise in his shallow breathing. Why didn't he press his lips against her skin?

"Nothing will keep me from you," she boldly managed to say.

Luka released her as he glanced down to search for her hand and clasped it. "Showtime. Follow me."

Holly obediently flanked Luka unable to believe her good fortune. As they walked along the crowded corridor, she was caught up in the vortex of backstage life. She observed his unending talents and knowledge of every facet behind the stage. He was impressive, and she was used to masters in their field, as was her fiancé, Brett, at the Templeton law firm in Beverly Hills, Luka Hunter was the best of the best. Everyone listened to Luka, waited to obey every command. Now, she too waited patiently to fulfill his every wish.

"I will take you upstairs in a few minutes to meet the lads. CMT wants publicity shots with video footage of you tonight and over the next few days. Have you ever been videotaped?"

Holly noticed Luka's sky blue eyes-to-die-for flashing with a discernable glint. "Depositions with clients, nothing with a budget like music videos." What Holly didn't say was she had been televised in hundreds of millions of households, all over the globe during the infamous Mason Collins murder trial that had been monitored gable-to-gable on television and satellite. There she had faithfully sat behind Brett Templeton, the lead attorney, supplying his every need.

Luka squeezed her hand and climbed the crowded stairs. The stairwell curved, and plunged them into a packed area that forced her back up against the wall, pulling his rock solid frame with her.

His breath quicken as she relaxed her hips against his. Luka slipped his brown leather clad hands around her waist and she tilted her head to rest her chin on his shoulder to drink in his masculine scent. Luka twisted his body to check each direction. The motion caused his chest to rub against her breasts, and the electricity, that flew between them, captured his attention. His lips brushed against the tip of her ear. "You feel so good."

"So do you," she spoke quietly, sliding her hands within his coat. She paused and looked up to Luka.

He looked down again.

They locked onto each other's eyes.

Her lips were only a breath away from his. Dare she press her lips to his? What would she do with all the desire that blazed inside her?

The passing crowd decided for her and pushed him into her. Locked in Luka's embrace seemed so natural, so proper, as he slid his leg between her thighs to fit perfectly against her. She draped her body over his as if she were a length of fine silk. The magic flashing between them seemed to make him experience the same feelings to get closer as Holly took a breath and relaxed against him. The warmth and the sweet scent of his masculinity drenched her.

As the crowd continued to press, Luka straightened his back to repel the pressure behind him so he would not crush her. Holly continued to stare into Luka's dreamy eyes. The electric blue of them dazzled her, as she fell into rich, inviting pools of adventure. Seductive eyes that dared her to stay with him blazing eyes that loved to gaze at her, impatient eyes that would swallow her whole if she'd let him.

*Mmmm, Luka Hunter, how had this delicious miracle happened?*

He blew a wave of words into her ear. "We have to move toward the dressing room, not much time left."

She nodded concentrating on his deep, tone of voice, which soothed her ragged nerves like a shaman's tonic.

Luka protectively gripped her hand and inched down the corridor fighting against the current of traffic. He arrived at a door and stopped at the same time as a tall, scrawny, unkempt man with an electric guitar on his back. Sweat beads poured from his brow, and large wet circles marked his wrinkled T-shirt. Happy to see Luka, he leaned in to say, with a thick English accent. "Hey, mate. Your fucking set list played great. Thanks again, I'm glad it's fucking finished. The pressure, to open for *Hurrikaine,* is fucking impossible."

Luka smiled graciously. "You were the only choice to warm up the hometown crowd."

The man was boney and had harsh features like a caricature of the skinny, homely Ichabod Crane. He asked Luka.

"She with you?"

"Why?"

"Not your usual beauty, but she has big knobs." He praised staring hungrily at her chest and lifted his glazed eyes to stare at her.

"Are they yours?" He gave her a leering wink as his hand reached out to touch her breasts.

Appalled, Holly instinctively stepped behind Luka.

"Mind your manners fucker, or you'll find yourself playing pubs."

"Hey, mate. Fucking touchy tonight. Opening night jitters?"

"I don't *get* opening night jitters' fucker!"

The obnoxious man shook his head. His long strands of narley, brown hair were soaked with sweat beads, and as he moved, splattered them all over Holly and Luka.

Luka turned. "Don't mind him, he's pissed and..."

Holly interrupted, not understanding his choice of word "pissed." But it was more embarrassing for Luka to explain.

"I get it."

Luka took her by the hand and squeezed it to show her he didn't agree with the ill-mannered rocker. Luka slipped his arm around Holly's waist and pulled her back out against the tide.

But the disgusting rocker's words lingered swirling like a ricochet in the shadows of her mind.

*Not your usual beauty.* Whom was she fooling? A drop-dead gorgeous man in Luka's position had the pick of all the beauties he wanted. She was no more than an assignment to him. Hadn't he called her a stupid, fucking, contest winner? Holly was aware enough of rock music to understand Luka assumed he was entitled to have a bit of fun on the side with her. Why not? She had gone for him in a big way, shamelessly throwing herself at him. Well, things would change — fast. After all, this was a business arrangement, and she would carry out her contest obligations, and back away from Luka as gracefully as possible. She straightened and squared her shoulders.

She had a plan.

Chapter Five

# BACKSTAGE PASS

Holly arrived at the top of the stairs. Luka clipped the gold, *all-access* backstage pass with the black and purple *Hurrikaine* logo to the lapel of her jacket.

"No one can stop you now," he confirmed. He smiled and winked at her.

Holly followed him down the long, congested corridor to another crowd of young girls dressed in skimpy black lace and leather. Their dull hair was dime store black, and their faces wore heavy black eye makeup.

Luka came to a stop. A devilish smile curled about his lips as he leaned close, and with a low, throaty whisper she would expect from him, shockingly confessed. "I'd love to see you dressed in black lace."

Holly raised her eyebrows and blurted out, "Black lace?"

How unfortunate, knowing she hadn't enough time to pack any black, lace lingerie. She quickly realized that she was dressed too professionally in the white suit and red camisole. She'd thought little about wardrobe for a rock concert when she'd packed. The firm had held her up with last minute details and she'd almost missed her plane. Sighing, she remembered why she'd left, to get away from Brett, and his demands to set a date. It wasn't true love, but the long-time-really-good-friend-that-saved-your-life kind-of-love, but not the way she should gush about a husband. A chill ran through her. Would there come a day when she denied Brett? Admittedly, being with Luka, she had dropped thinking about the awful decision if only for a little while.

She'd forgotten her plan to back away from the magnetic Mr. Hunter and she held tightly to Luka's leather-clad hand.

Luka dismissed the groupies, provoking snarls, and more poor attitudes, which took aim for Holly. She was learning to be on Luka's arm provoked strong reactions.

One girl challenged, "Who's that, Luka? Your boff for the night?"

Before Holly responded, another spoke up boasting.

"I'll bet I sucked you better than that slag will." She turned and looked at her pack of gutter-rat friends for their rallied approval.

Surprised by the outburst, Holly's cheeks flushed red yet was determined not to let them get the best of her. It was she that was going in on Luka's arm, leaving them at the outside door. She hoped things wouldn't get worse inside the inner sanctum of the rock star hideaway.

Luka was pulling her closer saying, "Don't listen to them. Pure envy of a beautiful lady like you. Stay close, introductions will be soon."

Unfortunately, the dressing room was not any better. Her beer buzz was fading fast, leaving her to crash drastically just when she needed to be relaxed when meeting the infamous hard rocking band, *Hurrikaine.*

Looking around, she thought the room looked like a gritty barroom scene in a B-western. Trashy well-wishers and adoring fans lined the walls, and she could not ignore the scantily attired saloon girls. Nothing in criminal law had prepared her for the hardness of music outlaws. And she made no mistake. These were filthy rich outlaws.

*Hurrikaine* and entourage were holed up and hiding out from the media and fans that made them fugitives. There was no doubt, how wealthy, they were. Holly appreciated the expensive guitars that lined a rack. Along another wall was the first-class buffet table gluttonously demolished.

"Where is he?" Luka demanded, turning on his heels as he raised his head. The room fell into a hush. Luka Hunter had spoken. He pointed to one scantily attired girl.

She quickly answered with a rough New York accent.

"Down the hall getting his cock sucked." She laughed adding. "I mean getting the rock star treatment." A nasty grin followed, pleased she'd delivered this raw bit of news.

No one seemed to care. Luka's face filled with disgust, and he shook his head as he started to explain. "He's...."

Holly cuts him off quietly muttering, "I understand. He's romantically involved."

"I doubt any romance is involved," Luka said with a snarl curling around the corner of his lips.

The raccoon-eyed girl sarcastically agreed. "Getting his cock sucked by a line of chicks' ain't my idea of romance either."

Holly closed her eyes, unable to get used to the crudities

of rock music.

"It's okay," Luka apologized as if he was a bit uncomfortable. He stared harshly at the girl and pulled Holly closer. "I wouldn't expect a lady like you Holly, to understand rock groupies. I'm glad I'm out of here in a few weeks." Luka continued to lash out saying, "Watch your language, a lady is present. Can't the lot of you bloody well conduct yourselves in a proper fashion? Looks like you all went 'round the bend," as he gestured toward the trashed buffet table.

Far from a corner of the room came the parroted phrase.

"Conduct yourself in a proper fashion," a male voice mimicked as if calling Luka out at high noon. The voice continued, "This is rock 'n' roll Luka, not a fucking tea party. You've been working at your fucking posh job at CMT too long."

Everyone laughed hardily.

On the outside, Luka took the joke well, half-smiling at the gathering, but his hand trembled as he tightly held hers.

"Come on, you can meet the band later." He insisted.

Judging by his cool demeanor Holly expected this wise ass would lose his job. And that the man would be dead if Luka carried a gun.

Luka led her out into the jammed corridor, pulling her close, weaving in, and out of stacks of equipment, heading deep into the belly of backstage. He twisted around the endless ten story scaffolds, farther away from the crowd, and even farther away from the lights.

Finally, all alone, Luka stopped, turned, and leaned Holly against a tall stack of trunks. A single ray of golden light, from a backstage bulb, spilled down to kiss the top of his golden hair.

Luka raised his leather-gloved hand and bent his fingers. He stroked her cheek like caressing expensive fabric. Her name rode the gentle wind of his breath, barely a whisper. The warm scent of his minted breath swirled so closely to her lips.

Their first kiss, so close, so evident.

# Chapter Six

# LET IT RAIN

**W**ould she find the strength to keep her knees from buckling? A few seconds passed. Luka's breath blew gently against her lips — his words unclear. *Turn off that sound!* Luka's lips came closer. What was that annoying sound? Why was he holding back? *No. Not now.* Not when her passion ran so high for him. *Don't leave me alone.* She pressed him, forcing her breasts against his chest, wrapped her leg around his. Her arms encircled his waist, and she thrust her hips into him. But nothing stopped Luka from pulling away.

"Holly ... Holly." He said intermittent, between short breaths. He weaned himself from her with a flurry of snowflake kisses from her cheek to her ear.

"My mobile."

*Mobile?*

What? Mobile? He made no sense. He pulled farther away and drew his phone from the pocket of his coat.

"Hunter." He snapped, his tone sharp. His facial

expression quickly grew with concerned.

"Fuck! You can't let it happen. We're ready to film this fucker as we speak. Stop them now. No ... I'll be right there." Luka's pinched eyebrows showed it all. "I've got to leave." He clumped his fingers to rub the temples of his forehead, ran his fingers through his hair, hooking the scarf, stuffed it in his pocket, permitting his hair to swing freely about his face. "I'll take you to where you can see the show," he stated flatly.

Apparently, nothing, she could offer, would influence him, but Holly didn't care about any stupid rock concert.

"Luka...." Her voice trailed with an impatience that surprised her. Her eyes told the actual story, glazed with passion and filling with millions of ideas fighting to change his mind. She relaxed, knowing he was leaving, and grumbled. "I know ... midnight."

He leaned and quickly kissed her cheek while his hair fell like shimmering threads to the side.

*No good at all.* That chaste kiss would not wipe away her growing feelings of failure. Her body quivered. "Go, and don't expect mercy at midnight Mr. Hunter."

He cocked his head, his long golden hair lay against his cheek. A noncommittal grin had graced his face before he admitted. "I rather like the thought of being at your mercy."

"I won't go easy." She sassed back with a flat tone.

"I wouldn't dream of it."

Holly tried to force a smile to curl about the corners of her lips to act her age. "Go, I'll find my way back to watch the show."

Luka hesitated, his hands catching hers as his chin

dropped to his chest. "I am sorry."

Yes, Holly was sorry as well.

Luka squeezed her hands meaningfully, turned, and disappeared into the dark.

She listened to the clicking of his boot heels on the floorboards becoming softer and then faint until all that was left was the backstage hum.

So very alone.

Standing in the shower of a single light, everything surrounding her was pitch black, except for an equipment box with the word *Hurrikaine* stenciled a foot high on the side. She kicked the box. "It's always something," she announced loudly.

She sat down on another piece of equipment and allowed jet-lagged tears to spill while crashing from the buzz of the potent English ale. Now bored, she was tired of longing for Luka only to have him turn away. The child inside her wanted a hug, to be held, and told everything would be all right. The woman in her wanted to be very close to Luka.

Lifting her chin, she noticed a soft melody. It was one of her new favorite songs, *Moments of a Memory*. She was surprised to realize it was by Hurrikaine. The melodic line was faint at first. The acoustic chords were plucked on a single guitar as if to soothe her abandoned heart. The beautiful love song grew louder and she started to hum along....

"If you'd let me kiss you, I promise, I will never leave you." Spoke a sensual male voice.

Holly straightened her back. "Who's there?" She inquired softly.

"Luka must be losing his touch." The reassuring voice mocked.

Startled, then embarrassed, she demanded. "Why didn't you make your presence known?"

"What, and miss Luka in all his glory? I think not. And he's a black-hearted scoundrel to leave you in tears, and unattended this way."

Holly wiped away, falling tears. His voice was calming, and she wondered whether to be mad at the intruder or not. She was too tired to fight with him too, so she took him into her confidence. "So what do you have to say about Luka's touch with women?"

"More than I want, I assure you."

"What makes *me* so different?"

"Well, let's say Luka's a bit of a tramp when it comes to the ladies. You, My Lady, well, you're not his usual."

The insulting words flowed back to tap dance across her sagging self-esteem — *not your usual beauty, not a beauty* — as hot tears spilled again, and she silently wiped them away.

The voice pierced the darkness, gentle, with a heavy dusting of compassion. "I didn't intend to upset you."

"You haven't." She softly promised.

"I can see I have. I meant...."

"Don't explain." Not again, the painful explanation, pointing out she was not a rock groupie, and would never be. What had happened to her plan?

The voice spoke softly as if measuring every word.

"You're too classy for Luka. You're a princess, and he's a troll."

"A troll? Luka Hunter? He's hardly a troll." She choked back a laugh as a tiny smile grew into a gentle giggle. The voice had gained ground. He was making her forget. The sounds of the climaxing guitar chords became louder, changed, and leveled off to quietly serenade them. Holly drew back a long lock of her waist-long hair, peering into the darkness.

"So ... you work for the band?"

"Something like that."

Holly leaned in to inspect her companion. She noticed a little trace of a silky British accent that was easy, but mostly friendly. From where she was standing, it was impossible to get a better position to see him. She sat and then scooted to the edge of the equipment box to see he sat with his side to her. He masterfully continued to pluck the beautiful melody on the silk and steel strings.

Holly peered past the outskirts of the light. In the dim glow, she saw broad shoulders, rounded and relaxed. His shiny, brown hair pulled back into a tail, and except for an annoying thick lock that hung to block his face, he was perfect. His two-inch sideburns blinked through a chin length lock as he swayed his head back and forth to the melody. The stranger was wearing a dark purple, silk shirt, with a banded collar. And as he turned to readjust the guitar that rested on him, a black Levi-clad leg came into view. His custom-made black boot was perched on a piece of equipment. Without notice, he stood, and she moved another inch closer, enabling her to see his open shirt exposing a slight amount of dark hair. She thought he was dressed expensively for a roadie.

He stopped playing and wove the guitar pick between the strings at the end of the neck. He gingerly leaned the instrument against something in the blackness. The border of the light revealed a beautiful, vintage Martin guitar. A long lock of defiant hair fell quickly covering his face. Her eyes drifted down his form-fit Levi's to the area that concealed how much pleasure he could give.

*Not again? Why was sex the first thing on her mind these days?*

The man stretched his back. He was tall, despite the fact that the darkness swallowed his upper body. He bent again and picked up the guitar by its neck with the gentleness of holding a newborn. A ray of light shined down on his straight nose, spilled onto his pale cheek along the square line of his jaw and over his perfect heart-shaped lips that parted to show incredibly white sexy teeth. He wore a full smile and surrounding his mouth, dimples to drive any female nuts. The scene left her riveted, breathlessly waiting, moment-by-moment, for him to expose more, and more, of his striking silhouette.

He stood and stepped closer to her. His unique blend of cologne was inebriating, luring her, pulling her to him, and as if she was falling, she wanted to reach out and catch hold of this dream weaver before he evaporated. A thin streak of light cut across the bridge of his nose. She should have been looking into his eyes, only he wore thick, black Ray Ban shades.

*Who are you?*

He seemed like he might be another gorgeous man. She looked at his arm when he lifted the vintage guitar. His deep purple shirt sleeve was rolled up once exposing a light dusting of dark hair against his pale English skin. As if he'd read her mind, he bent his long, delicate fingers and gently brushed her cheek wiping away a tear. His touch was tender and comforting. He was telling her everything would be all right. She was safe, for now, with him.

She jumped as a sharp, piercing roll of a drum set cut into her, invading their magic spell.

The handsome stranger flicked his head back, and the darkness swallowed his face. His hand slid along the line of her jaw to cup her chin as his thumb glided across her lips so gently, tracing the edge of her lip. "I've got to go, My Lady. Promise me, no more tears over Luka." He hesitated as if he didn't want to leave her, lifted the guitar, turned, and disappeared into the darkness.

*He called me My Lady again. How elegant he is.*

A new emptiness filled her as she listened to the sound of his boot heels clicking on the floorboards echoing in the distance. She watched his silhouette on the boundary of the darkness when he passed under an overhead stage light.

She was strangely alone.

Another music outlaw.

She watched him pass under distant lights, the guitar slung on his back.

*Mmmm, a fine looking outlaw.*

# Chapter Seven

# ROCK YOU LIKE A HURRICANE

**H**olly peered out from behind the stage as eighty thousand people stood chanting one name, *Hurrikaine*. Her head reeled from the deafening incantation, but mostly from the smoke that streamed from a machine a few feet away from her. She hated the smokes scent and the small, stifling VIP pit. To add to her torment, the frontman, the main attraction, was hidden by stacks of equipment.

Whoever said backstage was the place to be? Forced to settle for images of the back of the singer, draped over his microphone, she listened to him bewitch his audience. The omnipotent presence of him seduced her with a full-bodied voice that explained love to her hollow heart. It was as if he alone held the secret, the magic potion it would take to own her — heart, body, and soul.

This man never stopped to ask permission but took full

command of the arena. To her delight, she was becoming a willing participant in a conversion, something like a religious experience. Along with eighty thousand people, the *Hurrikaine* captivated her, as his rich, seductive voice persuaded her to follow him — into war, into the fire, through the gates of Hell.

After the concert had ended, Holly sat shell-shocked from the loud, pulsating speakers. *Hurrikaine* did not return for the customary encore. When nothing but smoke lingered on the empty stage, she tried to shake the disturbing emotions she'd entertained about the singer. Bits of intimidation teased her, knowing she would meet him shortly. Two and a half, incredible hours had passed, and she needed to gather her wits about her, find Luka, and leave the arena.

From around the corner, a young, red-haired, pimple-face man approached her. "Are you Holly Hill?" He asked with a German accent.

"I am."

"Mr. Hunter suggests you return to the city with your driver, and he's instructed me to say he will meet you as planned."

Holly stood shaking her head.

*Not again?*

She understood these types, like Brett. Their high profile jobs demanded them twenty-four hours a day. Her influence was limited and nothing would change that. She was left with spicy dreams of what it would be like to wake up with those dreamy blue eyes of Luka's hungry for her.

Holly's imagination swirled with vivid images as she took out the plugs from her ears Luka had given to her those last moments together. She cursed him for his continual thoughtfulness and dropped them into her pocket as she cut through the backstage security line to find Howard.

Settled back in the Bentley, Luka was on her mind. She'd found a man, but he was five thousand miles from home, and he babysat spoiled rich rock stars. She checked her watch again. Shortly she would see him, touch him.

Holly left a message with the concierge for Luka to meet her in the dimly lit bar. She sat in a seat far in the rear. It was late, and the attendant told her they would shut down soon, so she ordered a glass of red wine and dreamed of her long night ahead with Luka. She finished her drink and ordered another. She was checking her watch for the fifteenth time when the burst of cold wind blew into the bar announcing Luka's arrival.

"I'm late. It was impossible to get through the concert traffic, nasty business," he stressed expressing regret.

"You're doing fine." She praised as she sat back in her chair, fascinated by the sight of him.

It was so true. The tiny lamp's light confirmed Luka to be the most beautiful man she'd ever seen. He sat quietly, sprinkling his enchantment about her like magic fairy dust, pulling her into his spell.

Without breaking his stare, Luka moved his chair, oh, so close. His mint-scented breath caressed her cheek as the butterflies rose inside her stomach. "I couldn't wait to get to you. There were so many annoying problems. I finally walked out. Otherwise, I would have missed you." He explained, slipping his gloveless, warm hand under hers to hold it gently.

"I thought the bloody concert would never end. Not one of *Hurrikaine's* best I might add. First concerts are always rough. More of a glorified sound check to test all the levels and lights. Then some lout in accounting decides to start filming the documentary segment tonight to break in new video equipment. Of course, pieces were missing. Yet everything's supposed to be perfect. Impossible in rock music. All, I ask for, are the guitars be in tune, and the songs end when they're bloody well expected to end. Three more concerts and I'm out of here." He dropped chin to his chest, and his beautiful blond hair cascaded down to sweep the tabletop.

She shut her eyes as the sweet perfume of his hair made her lean in closer to inhale a deep breath of him.

Luka gently squeezed her hand and smiled.

Holly opened her eyes.

"Forgive me. I didn't intend to burden you with my rotten luck. I promise, straightaway, we will bask on the sands of California in the warm sun," he assured, glancing up to pin her eyes. Only for some reason his eyes had lost some of their usual confidence. They were exhausted and red-rimmed, yet an indefinable radiance sparkled whenever he looked at her.

Luka moved his attention to the passing server, turned on his charm, flashing a persuasive smile. "Miss, please, a mineral water, lots of ice?"

Holly watched the young woman process Luka's request as everyone she had seen him meet. Although they had officially closed, Holly suspected she would have moved mountains to fulfill Luka's order. Didn't everyone please

Luka?

Luka sighed and leaned back. He pulled a long strand of his hair back. He looked at her and smiled fully. A thought had crossed his tired face before he leaned in inches from her, so close, to convince her to forgive his earlier misdemeanor of leaving her alone.

She leaned in wanting to kiss his lips, to taste of him.

But Luka hesitated, his eyes narrowed. It wasn't hard for him to read her mind. It looked like she would get her wish. Holly almost closed her eyes to await their first kiss.

Luka cleared his throat and informed her. "Today, I have to work at the Hard Rock Café. We're filming a music video for "Now That I've Found You," the band's latest single off the *Illusions of Self* album, I'm here to promote for CMT. I have a never-ending list of preparations to check. My rotten luck, my job never ends."

Luka's mineral water with a twist of lemon arrived as expected, and he swiftly swigged it down as Holly realized what Luka was trying to tell her. He was a man in a hurry. He would leave her to sleep alone.

*No* rebounded in the secret place in her mind. "You're leaving?" she softly asked, but not sure, hoping to blot out any disappointment in her voice.

Frustration sprang into Luka's eyes as he nervously stroked each of her fingers as if to drive her wild. "I'm sorry," he spoke in a quiet, silky tone.

She was confident he used it to make sure women did as he wished.

"It's not what I want either, your first night in London to be alone. I'm not very chivalrous. But I have another two hours of work ahead of me *if* I'm lucky. I must be because I've met you. I'd invite you to join me, but soon the jetlag will crash in on you, and I'd rather you be fresh later."

"Later? What do I have to do later?"

"The video shoot. Aren't you aware that's part of your contest winnings, a guest shot on the video? And, I need your gorgeous face rested." He stated as he slammed back the last of his mineral water. "Breakfast before showtime?"

The compromise was breakfast. No late night of his hands caressing her skin. No soft morning lights to highlight his face. Only breakfast!

She volunteered in a calm, even timbre. "You might have called me here at the hotel rather than coming out of your way like this."

Luka flicked a long section of his blond mane over his shoulder with his head and squeezed her hand tenderly. "I had to see you. I didn't want you to think I forgot... well ... I ...."

His cellular phone rang. His facial expression grew weary with each peal. He responded with an annoyed tone that signaled to the caller it had better be important. "Hunter...." He listened with impatience while he idly played with the tips of her fingers. "No ... don't do a thing until I get there. Send the bleedin' fax. They will trust me on this one, or I'm out!"

Holly watched Luka control his frustration as he pushed the antenna down on the phone without saying goodbye. He opened his briefcase and dropped it into a pocket. Luka looked up at her apologetically, his baby blue eyes narrowed, and weakened as he looked at her. He pulled back a lock of his hair, took a deep breath, and slowly exhaled. He was obviously stalling. "I'll do what I have to, but I promise, tomorrow night you won't sleep alone. For now, I'm sorry. I'm needed."

"Luka?" She blurted, like what about our plans. Holly turned her hand over and reached out to hold him. He looked at her, the sparkle in his incredible eyes fading.

"Luka," she repeated, softly, as she would when the morning sun was caressing his face.

Luka closed his eyes quickly to make it clear this was as difficult for him. When he opened them though he appeared none the happier.

"In a few hours? Breakfast." What she didn't say was she needed him too. The moment was awkward, how to let go? She wanted to hold him, to kiss him.

But Luka's baby blues said he understood. He leaned over placing his hand gently behind her head and pulled her face a breath away. The sparkle in his eyes dimmed. He continued to stare deeply into hers.

She saw the pink tip of his tongue dart out to polish his lips before her eyes closed. A gentle, warmth washed over her as his soft lips tenderly pressed hers. His kiss hesitantly, a mere introduction, telling her he wanted more, but he didn't dare.

Swept away by the sweetness of his act of affection, Holly fought the urge to return Luka's kiss more forcefully. Her heart was pounding so hard she had no room to breathe. She wanted to kick aside the table between them, and wrap herself tightly around him, to deepen the kiss and mark her forever his.

Instead, he lets her go. Without looking at her, Luka bent, picked up his briefcase, straightened his shoulders, walked out of the bar, and never looked back.

# Chapter Eight

# SMOOTH OPERATOR

## Day 2

After a long, luxurious bath, Holly relaxed and sat naked on her bed. She was combing the tangles from her long hair when the telephone rang. "Damn it," she said, twisting her elbow as she reached for the receiver irritated she wasn't able to screen the call. She'd be forced to start her second day in jolly London, with Brett's angry voice admonishing her, for breaking the cardinal rule — always respond to calls. She took a deep breath and exhaled slowly. To her surprise, a smooth voice inquired.

"I trust you slept well? I didn't, my every thought was of you!"

"Luka? Tell me," she said in a sexy tone

"When I see you."

"You're sweet. Where are you?"

"Downstairs."

"Oh, I'm not dressed yet."

"Smashing, stay as you are."

A large, satisfying grin graced the sides of Holly's lips.

"I'm waiting," she challenged as if to dare him. She jumped out of bed, quickly brushed her teeth, and generously dusted her body with the hotel's lavender-scented powder, dashed to open her suite door, and left it ajar. She slipped between the crumpled sheets excited by the promise in his voice. Any second she would see his flashing blue eyes filled with raging desire.

Luka pushed through the door. He was heart-stopping gorgeous.

Her breath quickened as she drank in every inch of Luka. He was brilliant and utterly beautiful!

He never spoke a word, but flicked his dark blond, wet hair behind his back. His blue eyes flashed. They said it all. He was coming after her.

She wanted to squeal with delight as Luka crossed the room, dropping his cap onto the floor. His leather jacket landed with a thump. He pulled his black *Hurrikaine* T-shirt from his back, dropping it on the floor. He sat with his back to her near the edge of the bed, pulled off his boots, socks, and added them to the trail of clothes. He paused a moment. In her peripheral vision, she saw him unbutton the top of his Levi's.

He was ready.

Her heart raced with excitement.

He turned to gaze at her, and Luka's smile lit up the room.

She understood exactly what he was thinking. Would she do it? He was still technically a stranger. But she was stunned and overwhelmed by the glorious sight of him.

With a majestic wave of his hand, Luka pulled the sheet off her, and his foot kicked it to the floor while he stretched out like a beautiful sleek, wild cat.

She crawled across the bed to close the distance between them until she lay at his side. The clean, freshly showered scent of him set her body on notice, she was about to experience a blistering heat wave. Dizzy from his lusty entrance, Holly realized she never had a chance.

Luka beamed his seductive thoughts shining in his eyes.

"My turn — let me look at you." A sexy, boyish smile curled his lips, his radiant blue eyes continued to burn every inch of her flesh.

She relished being the center of his attention. If he made her flush with desire, with a single expression, she didn't dare imagine the joy she would experience when he was stirring her with his magic.

Luka laid his warm hand gently on the calf of her leg, and while inching its way up, he whispered, "Soft, smooth, as the velvet touch of new rose petals." He took a long, lusty, breath, and added. "You're so different, tender ... shy ... but so willing."

His assessment of her was music to her soul, but her cheeks burned. Embarrassed by her bold impulse, Holly squirmed to pull a corner of the sheet left on the bed up to cover herself. "Luka...." was all that tumbled out as she pulled on her bottom lip. She quickly fluffed her damp red-tinted hair around her shoulders to shield herself while pulling her legs up closer to her chest.

"Don't," he begged. "Don't hide your beauty behind

shyness for me. I can understand your shyness. It's a rare quality these days. It is often overlooked by the women I come into contact with daily." Luka stretched his arm out long, fanned his fingers, wrapped them around her ankle, and retraced his movements.

Almost giddy, but still self-conscious, from his slow caress, Holly straightened her back and curled her legs up more.

"Please, trust me. Let me see your muscles move, how your skin reacts to my touch. I want to watch as your long, silky, ginger hair falls to the side of your beautiful figure, and take pleasure in your breasts rising, excited by my touch. Let me enjoy you." He pleaded.

Instead of melting right there, she felt an unexpected, paralyzing confusion wash over her. But why? She wanted his touch. But the insecurities raced freely about her mind in circles, was she kidding herself? That after being with one man, so long ago, that she'd be able to handle this elegant world traveler. Nervously, she reached out to touch Luka's smooth, shaven face. With each stroke, she weakened, reading the message in his eyes that begged her to have faith in him.

Words followed to convert her.

"Please trust me. Your eyes say you want me. Your body says yes. Turn off your mind, forget your past, you're with me ... trust me."

She was too thunderstruck to speak. What an impossible thing to be asked to do! She searched his eyes, but how to trust him. His persuasive words matched the lusty firestorm flashing in his eyes. He was more overpowering than any daydream prepared her for, and her hand trembled as it cupped his chin.

He nestled into her palm as if he'd take anything she offered and pressed his lips leaving a moist trail. Luka closed his dreamy eyes, as he rubbed up and down the top of her leg, hungry for her touch.

*He was sooo fucking sensual.*

The devil himself couldn't have won over her any better. His face was relaxed, his eyes closing, becoming more angelic by the second. But he wasn't an angel. He was a man, and he was almost too perfect. She reached over, pulled on a long lock of his golden hair, and draped it over the tiniest ear decorated with a small, delicate, gold hoop.

Luka opened his eyes slowly.

She gazed into his, truly amazed. She didn't have worldly charms or much experience, and again, she questioned why he was here.

But here he was. Luka, with his lazy, sinful smile that was parting his lips.

Luka pulled his fingers through Holly's hair to reveal her breasts, causing his eyes to shine with joy. His fingertips traced the chasm down to the center of her chest, molding his hand to fit her plump mound, then down to caress her body.

He moved closer to nuzzle her cheek with his head. Swept her breasts with his scented hair and dropped down to lay beside her as he wrapped his top leg about her body. He started planting a long trail of kisses around each breast as if he was convincing her to come on an adventure with him. One she would never forget, and she forgot to stop digging her fingernails into her palms.

Luka's smooth, warm hand caressed the length of her, coaxing tiny bumps to rise in celebration on her skin. He spoke to her with the rhythm of his growing enthusiasm. He urged her to relax, enjoy, and let him touch her as he pulled his leg from on top of hers. He gently pressed her to lie on her back. Her legs uncoiled and straightened.

*Luka wanted all of her.*

Trying to accept him more easily, she wondered what exquisite pleasure he would intrigue her with now. His hair brushed her breasts with a light tickle. His warm lips dropped light kisses onto her shoulder like morning dewdrops.

She bathed in his words of praise.

"You're so lovely, so sexy ... you make me so hard."

She pushed her chest upwards watching him lust for her as he burned her flesh with his hot tongue. The sizzling tip followed the ridge of her breast up to the curve of her neck. His warm, powerful hand traveled down past her breasts to cover her thigh while his persuasive tongue searched her skin to mark every inch of her.

This man was no angel, and he was set to devour her. He pulled his hand along the inside of her leg, finishing at the top of her thighs, and slid his fingertips inside her.

She was biting her lip, drawing blood, and she didn't care.

His fingers spread apart.

His words were quiet, near her ear. "Open your legs a bit, let me in, please." The husky tone of Luka's voice slammed into her. "Trust me."

"Take me there." She surrendered and closed her eyes.

"I will if you'll let me touch you, let me kiss you, let me

taste you ... let me in .... I can make you fly."

Luka's words were powerful bolts of promise.

Searing desire shot through her like a hot flash. She slightly moved her legs apart for him and he set about to stroke her with lazy circles, repeating the movement until the sweet curling sensations beneath her belly slowly consumed her.

Luka whispered a few words, magically disarming her. "You're so soft, so wet."

The sensual words of this man drew her closer, melting her resistance, relaxing under his sensitive caress, and her legs opened more. Currents of hot, liquid lust followed his fingers as he penetrated her filling her. His thumb rubbed and coaxed the opening bud, and the electric rush made her groan from somewhere so primal she didn't notice.

Luka did and shoved his fingers higher.

Holly couldn't feel her cheek's flush, see how her skin shone with a light sheen from his masterful touch or the pleasure that curled around the corners of her lips.

Luka slipped in and out of her deep, wet valley exploring with his talented fingers, learning what pleasured her. Simultaneously, his mouth, his wondrous succulent mouth, ran across her shoulder, and up the long sensitive strip on the column of her neck. His tongue burning a long trail of hot sensations down her chest to fuel her scorching fantasies.

She twisted beneath him. Her breathing became more erratic as he nibbled on her hardening nipples. Joyfully trapped somewhere between Luka's sinful kisses and his intense lust, she groaned deeper. He was teaching her the way. He was showing her how to fly.

Deep moans slipping from Luka's throat, stirred more arousal in her, causing the floodgates of pleasure to open. He demanded her capture. His talented hands were overwhelming her.

Holly released a deep breath under his skilled touch.

Luka's breath became a searing flame over her breasts as he traveled upward to face her. His voice trailed so silkily, sexy, as he asked in a breathy tone, "Look at me."

Holly took a deep breath, unsure of what she would find and opened her eyes.

"Don't be embarrassed. I want you to understand, and feel how you excite me," he challenged as if to dare her. He pushed his lean, muscular hips against her leg, allowing her to feel the hardness of him.

*I can feel you.* She opened her eyes wider to find Luka's angel face so near hers. His chest brushed hers as he labored for breath, his sun-kissed chest expanded and the musky scent of his warm breath blew about her cheeks. Luka's full kissable lips close, so close, his eyes shining with a million possibilities.

For a split second, he scared her. Perhaps he was too much flesh-and-blood? She searched his incredible eyes, but what she found was his need for her. She relaxed and gave in to him. "I trust you, Angel Eyes."

That was what he'd been waiting for, dropping his luscious lips onto one nipple, sucking slowly until he went to the other. The rush of his tongue lapping and curling about her nipples forced any lasting doubts to shatter. Her fingers wove a pattern into the long locks of Luka's sun-streaked hair. Then like winding a rope, she pulled harder, as his tongue pushing her to the point of passion for him she'd never experienced.

He was lost in a fierce, primal rhythm with her.

Holly tugged his head back to taste his hot fiery tongue, which lapped, and suckled her breast as if he would never have enough.

Luka nudged her to spread her legs even more to invite him in deeper as if he insisted she crawl onto his hand. His wondrous fingers had never given up, dipping inside her, bringing her incredible pleasure. His plump mouth moved to kiss the base of each of her breasts as he straightened his lanky frame, pulled his body up and on top of her, and slid down her.

Luka looked up at her with those big blue eyes to-die-for and in a husky voice protested. "I can't do this if you don't let me. I want to please you."

She had never experienced what he was suggesting and now he was asking permission to drive her to madness.

Luka took her silence as the answer he wanted. His soft, damp hair draped about her stomach and down the sides of her thighs. She pushed the back of her head into the stack of pillows, rolled her fingers into balls, and closed her eyes not knowing what would come next.

Luka moved down, kissed inside her legs, creating a path, slowly, first one side then the other. His hands stroked the outside her thighs. He slipped them under to cup her derrière, pulling her up and closer to his lips.

Luka pressed his lips to Holly, kissing her tenderly. His lips parted and his velvety tongue introduced itself, bringing a warm gust of sweet lust. Like an overdue awakening,

Luka's loving drenched her, his special attention, lingering, teasing, and lapping at the tiny rosebud of her passion. Over, and over again, he plunged deeper inside her, probing, tasting, and sucking the trigger of her excitement, buried in a secret slumber. That is until Luka forced her arrival and awoke her with his extraordinary kiss.

Holly pushed back and cracked open her eyes, but she was blinded by Luka's escalating lust. She drew in a short succession of ragged gasps and tried to relax her feverish body. She couldn't control the broken sounds of her rising passion exploded from her throat, followed by violent shakes and shivers ripping from her head to her toes. Flashing white light splashed the underside of her eyelids. If she'd had one wish, it would be to live the rest of her life lost in this astonishing moment. "Luka, Luka...." She whispered throaty, almost a purr.

"Louder, Babe, I want my name on your lips. I want you to scream." He kissed her more deeply as if he'd known the private ways to satisfy her for thousands of years, knowing the perfect time to push her over the edge, and make her fly. He alone would deliver the special pleasure, the gift as the pureness of his lips moved with the same agonizing rhythm as his tongue.

Surely, it wouldn't be long before she flew her first flight.

Her body rocked violently.

Her head thrashed back and forth.

Paradise was in sight.

*Mmmm,* "Luka."

She fell from the edge, dropping, and flew into his chasm of pleasure, elated by the continuous waves of exploding joy.

"Luka," she whispered soaring in the clouds, floating in the bliss as she fell into a divine rhythm with him.

Somewhere far in the distance a sound wouldn't stop.

Luka crawled up her moist body to press his lips to Holly's, kissing her gently. His lips parted, and his velvety tongue slide in again signaling the end of the overdue awakening. Luka's fingers were skillful, caressing her every curve, showing her how special she was, completing her awakening.

The sound wouldn't stop.

"Please..." She broke away, drawing in an agonizing breath, recognizing what she was hearing.

"Don't answer."

# Chapter Nine

# LINGER

L uka was motionless as Holly careened from the edge. The waves of pleasure slowed to a stop. She forced her glazed eyes open and struggled to focus. She glanced over to Luka between heavily hooded lids. His body a perfect fit. She gazed into his eyes, but they were cold, and blue, staring back at her with no expectation.

The phone rang, piercing the silence — again.

"Don't...," she whispered as her blistering desire hung in a holding pattern.

He didn't flinch alerting her he'd stopped the unimaginable pleasure. "It's not my mobile. It's yours." He pointed out with a thick lacing of irritation.

The hotel phone rang again with agonizing annoyance while Holly threw her head back against the pillow. She fought like hell not to lose the high, but it faded, leaving her to wonder how much more of ecstasy would have arrived. But the ringing continued, squelching the moment.

"Answer it, Holly," he demanded tersely with a crisp edge

that now matched his eyes.

Holly reached for the receiver as if blind and placed it against her ear. She tried to calm her breathing and swallowed to steady her voice. "Hello?" she spoke with as much enthusiasm as her muddled mind mustered.

"Mr. Hunter's car is still waiting." A distorted voice stated.

Click. The line went dead.

Her mind raced. His car was waiting? She shut her eyes and paced her breath.

*Stay cool.*

*Think. Why was his car waiting?*

Holly moved and rested on her elbow, signaling to Luka that the wondrous time with him had passed.

His eyes still filled with lust told her he wasn't finished as he slid away from her sweat-sheen, body. He stretched out horizontally on the bed, crossing his arms behind his head to lie at her feet. His angel hair covered half of his flushed face.

She pulled a breath, how incredibly sexy he was. His blue eyes made her tingle. But she wondered what was he thinking?

*Never mind, his car was waiting. His car?*

She shook her hair forward to hide the team of insecurities vying to flood her face. His car? Had that been a prearranged signal for him? Was this a morning romp, and then off to work, she wondered as her doubts overwhelm her once again.

Luka stretched his arm, and stroked her calves, kissed the tops of her feet, and placed a red-painted toe between his succulent lips.

Holly barely kept up her pretense. She fought the compelling surges of lusty sensations, which were demanding she throws herself into Luka's capable arms and send her growing insecurities to Hell.

Holly paused to think.

Luka kissed the top of her foot again and checked his watch. Was he wondering where his call was, the one telling him the car was waiting? That he needed to leave her. He scooted to the end of the bed and sat up shaking his luscious hair. It seemed to move in slow motion as if blown by a gentle breeze, then fell to the sides as he bent to put on his socks, and boots.

Pretending she had been listening to someone still on the line, she blurted out. "No."

The no, she meant for Luka. *Don't ever stop.*

Too late, so she returned to the pretend caller to finish her cover. "No, I won't be around this evening. I have plans to go sightseeing." *Let him believe he wasn't all that was on her mind.* She paused again, knowing if she carried this pretense on much longer, Luka was sure to hear the lie pounding in her chest.

Luka stood, stretched straight, and tall as his stomach muscles flexed under his tight skin, making her want to reach out, and stroke his flesh. She took a deep breath instead and studied his California sun-bronzed body. He shook his hair and pulled his fingers through to fluff. The curves in his back rippled, and his Levi's hung below a fresh tan line on his narrow hips. This man did not wear briefs or boxers. A trail of light brown hair ran from his belly to the top of his unbuttoned Levi's, teasing her. She squeezed in a fleeting wish that he would take one deep breath so his pants would fall to the floor. To her disappointment, he walked over to the refrigerator, pulled an orange juice carton from inside, and chugged it all. She watched him as if he'd discovered a new cure.

She remembered her cover and returned to the phone. "I promise." She announced and casually hung up the receiver.

*Good, Luka didn't suspect a thing.* She turned to face Luka, but he was gone. Holly closed her eyes and curled her knees up under her chin. She didn't move. She was barely breathing. Slowly she opened her eyes to find Luka standing close to the bed quietly watching her every breath. Had this man with the angel eyes been playing her? Was he entertaining the stupid, fucking contest winner? Would he be interested in learning she was biding her time before she married Brett? That she wanted him to don his body armor and protest her marrying the dreaded dragon, Brett.

"Luka." She insisted as she wrapped her hand around his wrist, forcing him downward to her as if he was the only lifeline in a raging tempest. Her eyes spoke more than her words explained. "Luka," she repeated, holding back a giant sob caught in her throat. Hot tears welled in her eyes with no way to hide them.

Luka knelt down on one knee. His breath blew softly on her cheek. His dreamy baby blues filled with concern. "Tell me what's upset you? You're trembling, luv. What is it?"

"Hold me." She insisted.

He was here, now, and as her pride became lost to the fear that this was a momentary fling for her too, she added. "See how you make me feel?" It wasn't a lie. His awakening kiss made her tremble, but she had known him less than twenty-four hours and was unable to expect anything from him. He was Luka Hunter, the man who had his choice of all the beauties he wanted. No, she didn't think he would be interested in her dilemma of whether she should return to Beverly Hills, and marry Brett out of obligation.

Luka's soft words broke into her thoughts. "Don't think I'm a cruel bastard. I see you, a lovely woman, want in your eyes, tenderness in your touch, so willing, I can barely stop."

"Then don't Luka ... love me." She invited.

"I can't."

# Chapter Ten

# CONSTANTLY CRAVING

S he pulled herself up to a sitting position on the side of the bed and coaxed him closer. She wrapped her legs around his waist, pulling him as close to her as the bed would allow.

"Neither can you. I'm expected at the Hard Rock Café, and you're expected later." Luka clarified.

"No." She protested in another whisper.

"I see the need in your eyes," Luka added tersely, "but I can't stay."

"My eyes? Now, tell me, Luka, do you like what you see in my eyes?" she asked a breath away from his lips, ready to kiss him deeply, passionately.

"Yes." He consoled as he exhaled slowly, and arranged his other knee to kneel. He pulled her to the edge of the bed, holding her oh, so close by cupping her derriere. He licked his lips as if he would swallow her if she encouraged him. "I more than like what I see in your eyes. You don't hide your honesty. That makes me wonder if I might begin again with you."

Holly relaxed with his surprising admission. Perhaps he hadn't designed a brief morning rendezvous with her. Perhaps he was like her and had been drifting alone forever. "I have more than a look I'd like to give you," she offered confidently. For the first time, in a long while, she believed her future might not be the wife of an influential criminal attorney.

"Soon, hopefully, tonight, you can show me no mercy," he promised.

Holly pulled herself closer to him to calm herself by crossing her legs behind him at the ankle. She lifted his chin with the tip of her bent finger. She would kiss his lips and show him how much she wanted him.

"I didn't want it to be this way." He insisted in a soft voice with a twist of regret.

Her eyes locked onto his. Holly's thoughts stopped as she leaned back, and with lightning speed, her fingers moved down his chest to the top of his Levi's and forced the zipper down quickly.

Luka broke away. His breath ragged. "Easy ... easy. Don't." He caught her hand in his, pulled it up to suckle on the tips of each finger, and spoke with gentleness while his eyes sparkled. "I understand how you feel, don't ever stop."

"Do my eyes tell you everything?" She demanded.

Did they tell him she had been waiting for a man, never dreaming it would be him to awaken the woman in her? To make her feel special, and alive? The reason she had not died that night on the cold floor seven years ago — him.

Luka leaned in closer, and he kissed her shoulder and

nibbled at her neck. When he slid his soft lips up to cover the lobe of her ear, he whispered, "Your eyes tell me I need to bring protection."

*What?*

Luka pressed his hot lips against her ear once more. Holly forgot his words, squeezing her eyes shut. Never, had she endured such delicious torture. He moved, allowing his warm hands to roam her breasts.

Her nipples tingled and hardened.

She opened her eyes and looked at his saying that he felt the fire of desire.

Unexpectedly, reason whacked her in the back of her head. She understood everything.

Shaking her head, she scolded him. "Damn! You are a black-hearted scoundrel! It wasn't the phone call. You never intended to make love to me this morning. You brought no protection and counted on me not to have any, and you were right. I don't think that way. I'm so embarrassed," she confessed dropping her gaze. She quietly spoke choking back tears. "It's been many years since I've been intimate with a man. I foolishly thought you were seducing me. I wanted you, but I never thought of protection." Hot tears welled because the hot stab of inexperience was humiliating. Luka had been controlling her, and as much as she didn't like that idea, he'd succeeded.

Luka kissed the palms of her hand's one after the other.

The phone rang again.

She instinctively tensed.

Luka's voice was smooth and calm. "It's okay. That's mine." He gently removed her legs from around his waist, turned, and stretched out across the carpet like a wildcat to reach for his jacket. He pulled the ringing phone from the pocket. He turned over on his side, propping one arm under the back of his head, crossing his legs at his ankles. His voice became distant. "Hunter. Speak. Smashing. As I expected. He'd bloody well have to agree. I'll handle it from here. I'll be there soon."

Luka was distracted on the phone, working out more details.

Holly showered again and dressed in white panties. She looked around for a fresh bra but didn't have another. She'd planned on a shopping spree in London, never dreaming a beautiful Mr. Hunter would fill her days, and now, hopefully, her nights. She decided what the hell and pulled a gray cowl-neck, cashmere sweater over her bare breasts. She felt deliciously wicked. She slipped on a pair of charcoal, straight-legged slacks, and her gray YSL heels. She grabbed a black leather jacket planning to shop after her errand.

Holly shamefully avoided her image in the mirror. Her behavior with Luka resembled a lost puppy seeking constant affection, and she decided to go back to her original plan to cool off and back away from him. She put on blush, lip gloss and fluffed her hair, hoping to boost her confidence.

When Holly returned, Luka stood dressed. His presence made her knees weak and her decision to cool off forgotten. Luka took her into his arms, and she wondered if she possessed the sexual allure to convince a man like Luka to stay with her.

"Don't give me those sad eyes."

He was right, and there wasn't any time left. She rested

her cheek on his chest and lifted her chin to place a kiss on his neck. She slowly moved up on her tiptoes for a light peck on his full, luscious lips. Her fever continued to run hot as she looked at him, and asked. "Luka, when we make love, I do want to make you happy."

"You have already made me happy." He maintained so cool, raising one eyebrow, and winked. "I will enjoy making love as you call it. It's been so long since I've been near a lady. It's been *fucking* for a long time. But with you, I will make love." With that, Luka dropped his lips to hers once more and everywhere his tongue touched he left a trail of fires. "Mmmm, Holly, how much I want you," he vowed between shallow breaths.

His body slammed into hers, the evidence of his arousal branding her to make her, his. She reacted with explosive passion preparing to kiss him senseless.

Luka broke away, pulling his Ray Ban sunglasses from his pocket. He slipped them on quickly as if to hide the glaze burning in his eyes. Too late, she'd seen the fire and the accomplishment made her smile.

"Ready? It's close to showtime," he announced, and his radiant smile lit up the room.

"You're absolutely beautiful," she confirmed under her breath.

Luka grinned as if he had heard her. *Maybe he had.*

Downstairs Luka politely took Holly's hand and escorted her to the waiting cab. She noticed the meter had been running, no wonder the driver had called.

Holly sat in the back with him buttoning her short, tailored, black-leather jacket, watching Luka. She noticed tiny smile lines forming around the corners of his eyes, as he smiled at her, making Luka older than her.

How had she found this amazing man with eyes that danced whenever he looked at her? She wondered aloud.

"I'm confused. You have a hectic agenda yet here you are."

He tenderly drew her to him. "You don't see what I do the most beautiful woman in this city. The question, you should ask, is how you can forgive me after I left you last night. Trouble is I handle everything that happens to *Hurrikaine* in London. Sometimes my work takes precedence over the desires of the heart."

"So ... I am a desire of your heart?" she asked, dazed by his romantic flare.

"You are my only desire. But with the production schedule as it stands, I have no free time."

*My only desire.*

Holly hadn't heard a good deal after his courting words because his eyes betrayed him, there was more going on inside than he was articulating.

Luka was mysterious. She could see he was very sharp and aware of where he was. And overseeing the band of wealthy outlaws had honed his skills. No back-sniping gunslinger would ever creep up behind him and shoot him in the back.

"How many await your return in California?" His direct question surprised her.

"No one I care to mention," she answered, knowing Brett Templeton was nothing more than a faint memory.

His face brightened, and Luka's answer told her he had no

one special waiting.

"Smashing, I promise you. We will watch many sunsets together."

She liked that idea because sunsets were the start of long evenings she hoped to devote to him. She sighed, realizing she spent most days locked away in stuffy courtrooms. Other days and nights, she'd hid away in the law library or hung out doing surveillance, following clues and investigating rumors. She was so dedicated she could turn Mr. Roger's life in the neighborhood into a criminal case.

Holly realized she hadn't been able to leave work to watch any sunsets for a long while. She looked at this man thinking how extraordinary it would be if they fell madly in love with each other at the same time. What a fantastic miracle that would be. *Yes, we will watch many sunsets, Mr. Hunter. You can bet your life on it.*

Luka asked the cab to stop at an out-of-the-way café. They ate a quick breakfast of Earl Grey tea, warm scones with orange marmalade and agreed she would tour the Golden Circle of London alone, promising to meet him at the Hard Rock Café by eleven.

He paid the check, handed her a few English pounds to pay the taxi fare, and left her standing disappointed on the street as he slipped into a black Hackney cab. Why hadn't he kissed her wildly?

*Okay, Hunter, sometimes you're affectionate, and others aloof, but you invariably leave me desiring more.* She watched Luka fade into the merging traffic, drawing in ragged breaths thinking about him.

She was utterly alone.

Any other day Holly would have skipped along the streets of London, overjoyed to find a wonderful man like Luka. But lingering thoughts of betraying Brett and the repercussions for not marrying him, were draining her joy and elation.

Holly stepped into a Hackney cab, apprehension, her strongest companion. She gave the cabby the address where she would collect the other reason for her London visit, the investigation for Brett's current case. An hour later, Holly faxed the expected research to her assistant Lucy.

With Brett weighing on her mind, she wondered, how to stop the grinding cycle of questions. She sighed heavily.

*Oh, Brett, so far away, so long ago, so many wasted years.*

*I don't love you.*

# Chapter Eleven

# SIMILAR FEATURES

Holly exited a lingerie boutique. She'd purchased a black lace thong and bra for Luka to rip off her at midnight. When Holly arrived at Piccadilly Square, she had *Hurrikaine* on her mind. She went into Tower Records, and as time was limited, she quickly browsed the *Hurrikaine* CDs section to gather a brief profile of the band.

She found five previously recorded CDs, many imports, and single CDs, along with the new release *Illusions of Self*. Dark-haired Kaine Walker, the only singer — was a sinfully, sexy, elegant man — the kind women would follow anywhere. He'd composed all the songs — except — she read on to find Luka credited with writing the all-time favorite love song "One Love." Stunned, she mumbled under her breath. "Luka writes love songs? For whom?" In a flash, one name popped into her mind — Carrin — the name he'd called her when they'd first met.

She busied herself for the next few minutes. She matched names with pictures of the band members and *Hurrikaine's* extensive song catalog was extremely impressive. She remembered the awakening she'd experienced while she'd listened to the songs at the concert realizing she had loved the singer's lyrics, and voice for years. Love. That man sang about what real love was, and he'd given her more hope that she could find it with Luka.

She checked the clock. Luka expected her soon for the new *Hurrikaine* video, "Now That I've Found You." She flagged a cab and directed. "Hard Rock Café." She nibbled at her nail tips with each passing block, her excitement growing until she was on pins and needles.

Her cab pulled up in front of a café with two brown awnings. There were no telltale signs that the world knew *Hurrikaine* was about to appear. A familiar smile caught her eye. Luka was peeking out the front window. In a flash, he came out to the curb to greet her. Was it possible he had grown more handsome? She fell into a fresh chasm of smoldering lust with him once more.

"Carrin ... Have a lovely morning sightseeing?" Luka spoke gently, sweetly, his bright blue eyes sparkling as he looked at her.

His words were sobering, might as well have thrown ice water on her lusty fantasies about him, and she was sure he hadn't realized he'd called her Carrin — again!

"Luka! I'm Holly." How intensely the embarrassment stung her cheeks. After their special morning in her bed, he'd called her another woman's name. She didn't know what to make of it?

"Of course, I know your name."

"You called me Carrin," she argued, fighting with a stray

windblown curl. The moment was awkward, would it ever pass.

A muscle twitched in Luka's cheek, he exhaled and conceded. "Oh, bloody hell, okay, you remind me of someone I once knew."

"Knew intimately by the tone of voice you use when speaking her name."

"You are perceptive, Miss Hill." A sexy smile curled around his mouth.

Now was the time to pursue this line of questioning, and find out, who Carrin was. However, Luka gained her sympathy when a flash of pain passed as a comet across his angelic face. Luka's weary blue eyes bore witness to the fact he'd hoped he'd covered the distressing memory.

She was glad he hadn't. Possibly someone else not trained to analyze the body language of the client might have missed the moment.

Who was Carrin — and how had Luka become such a lonely man?

He slipped his hand around hers and suggested. "Come with me lovely lady. Obviously, I have a confession to make, and it can't wait any longer."

She followed him into the café. Even the back of his body made her breathless.

Luka continued inside but moved to the left to give them some privacy. Something heavy was on his mind.

Holly struggled to maintain her wits about her as Luka pulled her into his warm, scented body, oh, so close. She grabbed a tiny breath and sighed raggedly as he tightened his arms around her waist. He felt sooo good, and he was setting her body ablaze again, luring her deeper, and deeper into his wicked spell. He slowly and calmly stripped her will from her, capturing her completely. Why was she so powerless when she was near him?

*Mmmm, Luka.*

His firm body, familiar, and inviting, his dreamy blue eyes-to-die-for were laced with so many possibilities. She would bet he was thinking of Carrin. She pushed the length of her body hard against Luka's reminding him he was holding her.

*I'm Holly touching you, not that ghost from your past.*

She knew about ghosts. How they ate you alive. They never let you do anything but live in the past while their function was to erase any chance to maintain an existence in the present and certainly obliterate any thoughts of a future.

Jealousy nipped at her resolve as she brushed her lips along Luka's smooth golden neck. She was purposely reminding him she was here, in his arms, flesh-and-blood, and wanted him closer. "Luka." She touched his lips with her fingertip. "My pretty long-haired pirate, look into my eyes and see how wonderful you make me feel," she instructed, as she studied his eyes, her words dipped in longing for him.

His body relaxed and clung to her. He took a deep breath as if he was going to explain, but said nothing. However, his body spoke volumes. He nestled his lips against the soft fold of her neck, and shoulder, still hesitant, holding back.

What stood between her and Luka Hunter?

Jealousy, so powerful, grew stronger and started to consume her. She selfishly wanted all of him, all his attention. She rested her chin on his chest, pressing her mouth against his neck, once, twice, three times. Seconds later, her stubborn pride prompted her up on tiptoes to press her mouth to his full succulent lips. "I'm Holly, Luka ... kiss me. You are *my* lover now," she announced fighting with everything she had to win him back from the potent memory. She must have shattered his resolve because, like a clap of lightning, Luka pushed her, slamming her back up against a wall.

His passionate fever confused her. His mouth opened, his tongue darted out, and he filled her mouth. He was kissing her deeply, searching as if lost in a memory he desperately needed. Whom was he kissing? Did it make a difference? Had fate twisted their lives together, creating a second chance for both of them? She couldn't think anymore. Luka's scorching outburst and husky tones of pleasure were rumbling in his throat, meant to unlock and release her inhibitions.

Holly returned his generous kiss, opening her mouth to welcome his hot tongue, and brushed it with her. She pumped his mouth, loving him, trying to show him it was she, not a ghost living among them. Whoever Luka was kissing, no longer mattered. She welcomed the confinement of his enraptured embrace.

His hand roamed her freely, about her back, in her hair, under her cashmere sweater. He slid his hand over her skin and lingered at the soft beginnings of her curves. His hunger flared, and his hands covered her breasts as he broke the deep kiss. "I love the soft feel of you, the fresh taste of you, and your willingness to please me." He praised into her mouth kissing her again, and again.

He caught a breath adding, "The lovely fragrance of your hair." He gently kissed her again. "Holly, I know I'm with you," he stressed heavy emphasis on the word you. His words trailed into another spellbinding kiss, then spoke softly. "Never doubt that."

Luka's fiery tongue devoured her again, hard, almost violent. His hunger swelled in his pants as he slid his leg between hers and rubbed his hips against her. His fiery touch shortened her breath until it vanished. Before long, she would pant, and after that who knew? No man had ever kissed her like this before leaving her barely able to think. Her hand traveled down the front of his Levi's to rest over his growing size. She instinctively responded with another hot, maddening kiss to tell him she wouldn't disappear. She knew the ache of losing a loved one in a fleeting instant. His kiss told her he had lost someone too fast.

Luka pushed his hips into the mold of her hand. His escalating lust urged her beyond a lady's endurance, coaxing her hand to move in long, quick strokes until he was strong. It was too late to control herself because her growing passion insisted it was time to taste the full size of him, to show Luka her excitement for him. She reached for the button at the top of his pants.

He kissed her, telling her what his promise was in the next few minutes.

Too soon, the loud clatter of the crew passing them violated their private world. As rapidly as Luka had begun, he broke the magic spell and pulled away. "Forgive me." He quickly apologized, and backed away catching himself, his tone full of regret, his words a whisper, his breath shallow. "I can't do this." Shaking his luscious angel hair, Luka's beautiful angel face was etched with anguish. His usually cool blue eyes imprinted with guilt and torture.

She wouldn't have expected this dramatic reaction from this man, so controlled, and confident. What was the overriding sadness, behind his blue eyes-to-die-for hiding?

Luka stepped back further no longer looking at her.

Holly tried to place a battery of tiny kisses down his neck while her passion stormed white-hot.

Luka glanced down at her and moved to keep his distance. He lowered his eyelids trying to hide his intolerable demons from her.

Too late, she had seen his unbearable torment again, and she knew the misery.

"Who was Carrin?"

He said nothing. Rather, he stepped closer to her, hugging her tenderly as if to comfort her. His hardness relaxed and his breath steadied.

Luka grumbled in a level tone of voice. "It happened long ago."

"What happened? Tell me your secret."

He squirmed and countered. "She's not a secret. She's ... I don't talk about her." As if he was thinking aloud to himself, added, "If there was a secret, it was, well ... Carrin ... we were together long enough for me to see myself getting married, raising a family. One day..." His body stiffened, and his voice cracked.

What the hell happened to Luka?

"Out of nowhere her bastard, ex-boyfriend came back for her. One minute we were in love, the next she was gone, taken from me."

She'd have never guessed any woman capable of leaving Luka, for any reason. She had a million questions, but his glistening eyes said he was finished with reminiscing.

Luka dropped his head back to give him a second to control his emotions. His neck stretched.

She found it difficult to restrain herself and not design a trail of kisses from one earlobe to the other. He needed her comfort now, not her passion.

"Forgive me. I had no idea I was still this emotional about what happened. I swear it was years ago. Still, something about you is familiar and makes me share my feelings. I'm usually too busy with work. But I'm here with you in a way I have long forgotten. I'll never be able to thank you Miss Holly Hill." He praised and pushed his Hard Rock baseball cap back on his head.

"I swore I'd never love any woman. Never endure that type of pain again. Never ... again," he vowed as the intensity of his voice rose. His eyes filled with fury, and he looked at her with his angel face, but his hard expression was softening. The gentleness in his eyes pierced her heart as he completed his sentence. "...until I saw you. I wanted to run away with you. I remembered the joys of love. The wonderful feelings of being in love and it would seem that you rekindled those feelings I abandoned a long time ago."

"You'd lost hope?"

"Yes. I won't lie. I've had my share of women and more, had all the sex I've ever wanted. But, love? I'd lost all hope for love in my miserable life. I've never believed in second chances. I never expected to be so happy to know a woman."

She smoothed away the stinging memories lacing his face as her fingertips traced his cheekbone and chin line.

A tiny, peaceful smile pushed his lips apart before he spoke, showing her his fabulous straight, white teeth.

"You're a bloody miracle."

Luka's words made her feel like they were whole as if they belonged to each other, one man, and one woman. Filled with happiness, she wrapped her arms around his waist and hugged him tight.

*What of Brett?* She knew Luka would handle it. Luka was talking about love and being in love. She wondered if it would be with her. Soon she would tell him her decision was made.

Luka held her and forever would not have been long enough. He took her hand and silently walked her into the main room of the Hard Rock Café with a beaming smile on his face. His ghost tamed — for the time being.

The walls, covered with rock music paraphernalia, displayed autographed vintage guitars, photographs, and advertising posters littered the stark background. The restaurant was empty save the twenty members of the video crew and their equipment.

Suddenly, Holly heard a loud, thunderous motorcycle approaching. Luka leaned over to explain into her ear.

"Kaine will ride it in another shot for this video. It's a clean machine, hard to find. It's called a Vincent Black Shadow." He boasted with a heavy dose of envy.

Luka gently released her and led her to the bar where he threw one of his legs across a stool and leaned on the bar with his elbow.

Holly slid onto the stool beside him. The crew scurried about preparing for the shoot. Holly wondered when Luka would tell her the rest of his story. Though she wasn't convinced, she wanted to know every detail.

"Something to drink?" he asked, his eyes saying he trusted she'd stop asking him questions, "I'm having a mineral water."

"Beer would be fine," she responded.

He accepted the order from the bartender and held out a long-necked bottle with a slice of lime wedged into the glass neck.

"I've never had beer with a garnish in it." She smiled generously.

"Well, you're with me, and now you're living the high life."

They laughed together, and it seemed possible they could become more than physically attracted to each other. He had shared a crucial secret with her. She wondered when it would be her turn. She invited the warm feelings of friendship building between them, relieved to be this close to him, and not fight the constant urge to rip his clothes off him. Still, she completely understood why all the women at the shoot shot a second glance over their shoulder to Luka, when he walked near them. He truly was striking, especially his angel hair that sparkled under the backlighting of the Klieg lights. His black *Hurrikaine* T-shirt that hugged his well-defined chest. His dark blue Levi's that matched his eyes.

*Mmmm, Luka.*

Luka crossed his leg and rested his ankle on his knee, exposing two-inch heels on the black alligator boots as he fanned his fingers to mold to the shape of her thigh.

Overcome with a new wave of lusty feelings for Luka, she impulsively slid off her stool and snuggled up close to him.

His arm instinctively slipped about her waist, pulling her to him. "What? Something wrong here? Need something?" he asked in a low tone of voice that caught in his throat.

"You. All of you." Who would have believed how free her words of swelling arousal flowed toward Luka? A simple look from his disarming eyes had transformed sweet, shy Holly from the firm, into an awakened woman. A sensual woman acknowledging her needs and wants for comfort, with an easiness she hadn't dared to express for seven long years, maybe never.

Luka's smoky blue eyes studied hers while he dropped his leg, slipped both of his hands around her waist, and pulled her between his legs. She could feel the warm curl of longing stabbing deep below her belly. Her eyes locked on his beautiful succulent mouth.

Without warning, the Klieg light above them went dead, spreading an instant dimness about them, inviting her to lean in, and kiss Luka.

His tongue darted out as the darkness fell like a cloak. He parted her lips and slipped his tongue into brush hers, then devoured her, filling her mouth. His kiss was brutal, forceful, tempting, letting her know she was playing with fire. He was telling her he was a man pushed beyond what he could bear. That she was driving him insane. Crazy with a mixture of longing, lust, and a twist of anger, because he couldn't slip away from there with her, and fill her with a burning, consuming hunger that was destroying him.

Holly couldn't catch her breath.

Luka's hand clutched the front of her neck, gripping her tightly, pulling her closer.

To show him proof of her arousal, she slid her hand up to the top of his thigh. She lingered, unsure how far to excite him, and decided to go for it, tracing the growing bulge in his pants. She heard his quickening breath.

He fought again to break away. "Please? I have to stop before I can't because we have no privacy. We have hours of shooting ahead of us." His eyes pleaded with her, he fought for his breath and shook his head no. "Being with you is twisting my insides. I can't take a whole hell-of-a-lot more of this."

"I can take all you have to give."

"Awe, Babe, please don't look at me with those eyes. What am I going to do with you?"

"Whatever your heart desires." She proposed, thinking he'd called her Babe. He was softening, giving her a pet name.

Luka shut up and raised his perfectly arched eyebrows to show he realized he would not win this round. He smiled his lazy, sexy grin. He spoke with a nervous laugh.

"Thank you. You do not understand how deeply your words affect me. Holding you, touching you, kissing you, I'm feeling all the same things you are. Only I'm afraid to let you see how much you tempt me."

Luka kissed her again with deliberate madness. "Holly ..." he whispered, so thickly, "I have to stay here. CMT expects me to direct this latest video and release it to sell more tickets abroad. Between wanting to fu — forgive me, make love to you, and my duty to CMT, I'm in an impossible situation. I have to say no to one of you."

"I know what I'm hoping." She encouraged dragging her nails up his thigh again, hoping to convince him, gripping a hand full of his growing arousal, and squeezed slowly.

Luka's breaths quicken. His body shuddered with groans of pleasure lodged in his throat. His mouth went down over her and kissed her deeply, wrapping one leg around her to ground her.

The blood pounded in her head, as his hands dropped to cover her derrière and slammed her hips into him.

Luka broke away from her like he was drowning, and out of air, and abruptly threw his head back. He gasped for another breath, stretching his neck until his hair fell to the middle of his back, dropping the baseball cap to the floor. Between broken breaths, he fought for words. "I'm not a sane man anymore, not since I first saw you. I lust for you. I can't bear the thought of not having you." His voice is weak, shaky, on the brink of breaking, and his eyes so dark they were almost black.

*Mmmm, quite a confession.*

His lips were wet and puffy from kissing her so passionately, and she saw them coming for her again. Luka's kiss told her he no longer wanted to fight her. That she was his weakness. Yet, for him, each breath became a battle. Holly could feel his reason warring with his body, trying to tell her he didn't want to, but he would leave — she knew which had won.

Determined to have Luka for a few seconds more, Holly

molded her hand to his hardness as the strokes became more frantic. She dropped her hand and thrust her hips into him, driven by a possessiveness that would have frightened her a few hours earlier, as she demanded he stay with her. She kissed him wickedly expecting him to crush her with the hunger of his passion.

He broke away from her first. Luka's hot breath blew into her face, in short, rhythmic puffs. "Somehow — I will make you scream."

Holly smiled, relaxed, pulling her hand away, and wrapped her arms around his shoulders. She placed her lips on his silky skin and kissed him on his tiny earlobe, down his neck, and quietly praised him.

"That's better. Don't think I won't hold you to that, Mr. Hunter."

# Chapter Twelve

# YOU'RE SO VAIN

L uka grinned allowing a mischievous smile. "No, mercy," he confirmed, and released her. It was showtime. Luka struggled to steady his breath while slugging back a few swallows of mineral water.

She'd lost the battle, but was confident she would win the war raging inside Mr. Hunter.

Holly ran her fingers as a comb in her hair to fluff it. The band was arriving, and she recognized the members by name from her Tower Records research, as they walked in one-by-one.

To her left, Ian Montgomery, keyboard player. Tall, and lean, his long blond, shaggy hair dripped down his black, silk Asset shirt, with black matching leather pants, and boots which made him look more like an undertaker.

When Ian turned, he spotted Luka. A warm smile penetrated his serious look. That is until he saw her. His eyes widened, and his face went completely ashen as if he was in the presence of a ghost. He looked at Luka, then to Holly, and stopped walking to stare with a look of puzzlement locked in his eyes.

Chris Taylor, the bass player, ran right into the back of Ian. He too was staring at her. He was medium height, lean, had long, light brown hair tied back with a dark purple scarf about his forehead. His clothes were more neutral. A torn purple *Hurrikaine* baseball T-shirt that read *Lose Your Illusions,* beneath an unbuttoned, black, leather vest, black Levi's, and black, leather boots. Chris spoke into Ian's ear with the same look of bewilderment.

Michael Evans, the drummer, joined the elite group. He was Ian's height, slender frame, with straight, dark, waist-length hair. He leaned in and pulled along an attractive young woman holding a clipboard. It looked as if he had been schmoozing with her, before Ian, and Chris distracted him, both stopped in a frozen posture at the sight of Holly.

She gazed at the handsome trio and muttered, *"Hurrikaine* is the best damn looking group of men I've ever seen."

Michael, dressed entirely in black, wore a three-quarter's length leather slicker, black Levi's, boots, and cowboy hat to complement his wealthy outlaw ensemble. Now, they all stood gawking at her.

One was visibly excited. "Wait until Kaine sees this," he said with no noticeable British accent.

"Is he here?" Another voice spoke as clear as a native Californian.

"Somewhere? His Grace was behind me." Another voice volunteered with a British accent.

Unexpectedly, Holly overheard a young woman from the crew to her left say full of excitement, "My God look at

Kaine! He's fucking smashing!"

Holly turned to look for him, but it was dark, too dark to see. She put a fingernail between her lips to nibble, hoping to calm the overwhelming anxiety building within her.

*Fucking smashing...*

Kaine!

Who would have guessed Holly from Beverly Hills, to have a cameo role in a music video with *Hurrikaine,* the top-selling rock band ever?

The words rock band sounded so misleading. The thick biography of the band that she'd quickly scanned at Tower Records stated they were in their early thirties. These men standing feet from her, staring at her as if they were witnessing the second coming represented the five top wealthiest entertainers in the world. Kaine being the songwriter was the richest. Considering the stockpile of wealth from a typical client of the law firm, that was pocket money to *Hurrikaine.*

A commotion at the door drew her attention, but not the crowd congregated in front of her. Nicky Jamison, the lead guitar player, was the last of the band to arrive. He joined Ian, Chris, and Michael. He too donned the 'who the hell is she?' look.

A cavalry of bodyguards flanked Nicky and he had the requisite good looks to be in *Hurrikaine.* Long, shiny, medium-brown hair with blond highlights, draped long over a black, silk tailored Asset jacket. His prominent rocker image insisted he dress in a pale purple, banded-collared shirt, black Levi's and black deck shoes, his ears were trimmed with gold earrings and wrists with bracelets. Tall and well built, he was the only one to stop his staring and headed directly toward Luka.

"Where's Kaine?" he asked with a deep, husky American voice that sounded like a well-trained radio announcer. He never asked the real question. Who was the lady sitting beside Luka? More to the point, why?

"Playing rock star. You know Kaine. I'd like you to meet Miss Holly Hill. She won the CMT contest. She's here to shoot the guest spot on the video." Luka explained as if to shut Nicky up before the barrage of questions in Nicky's eyes started.

Holly was no longer interested in her drop-jaw effect on these fine-looking rockers, she knew why she attracted their attention, but her curiosity about Kaine was growing stronger. Draining her beer, she ordered another, and when she turned around to drain it again, the cluster of men had disappeared. She sat the empty beer bottle down on the counter.

Luka turned and instructed. "Come along, follow me. I'll take you over to makeup and wardrobe."

She had to ask, "Luka, why were they staring at me?"

"You know."

"Carrin?"

He didn't even bother to answer.

Holly followed Luka out the back entrance toward a row of trailers, there he opened the door to one, and she stepped inside to find several people waiting for her.

"Praise be, thank you for sending me an angel," squealed a scarecrow of a man, bald, and colorfully dressed. "Hello, pet. I'm Peter, and I will have a perfectly lovely time styling your magnificent hair. Naturally curly I presume?" he asked confidently as he lifted her hand to kiss respectively on the top.

"Englishmen," Holly muttered under her breath though delighted.

"Your Ladyship," added Peter warmly in his thick cockney accent as he pointed to a raised chair in front of a wall-length mirror. He combed her long, frizzy hair that had been harder to control than usual because of the balmy English weather.

An attractive, fashionably dressed woman breezed in asking, "You're Holly, the model for the shoot?" She inquired with a thick British accent, origin unknown.

Holly's cheeks brandished a rosy blush that would last for hours. Her evaluation was quite a change from the critical rocker's remark backstage. "Thanks for the kind words, I'm not the model, but I am here for a guest shot in the video."

"I'm Lilly, here to make your dreams come true," promised the attractive, raven-haired woman, dressed in black, baggy sweater, and leggings with knee-high boots.

"Impossible ..." Holly replied with a wicked smile that curled about the edges of her lips.

"You're so right about that. That's my job." Luka confirmed nonchalantly.

Holly looked up to see Luka's reflection in the mirror when his blond head popped in the doorway. She found a glint of his undeniable hunger for her shined brightly in his clear blue eyes.

Lilly took a double take. "Is that a smile? Bloody impossible!"

Luka entered and playfully pushed Lilly with his hip. "I have something to smile about," Luka admitted as his baby blue eyes to-die-for locked onto Holly's.

"What brings you down into the trenches' Hunter? You might get your polished manicure dirty."

Luka laughed warmly, obviously comfortable with Lilly's teasing, and protested. "Not you too Lil? Can't a chap oversee a project without all this bloody resistance?"

"Not possible with you Luka, been a long time since you've come 'round to us grunts, especially after you went and crossed-over to CMT. But, now you're here. I don't think it will be difficult to dress her."

Lilly didn't wait for a reply from him and turned to Holly while Luka left the trailer. "Your first shoot?" she asked, placing color swatches against Holly's skin.

"Yes. It's all so exciting."

Lilly laughed and encouraged her with a warm smile.

"Relax Holly, with your bone structure, and gorgeous hair, the camera will love you."

*Relax. How was she supposed to do that?*

A second later Luka returned. In a demanding tone, he instructed Lilly. "A wardrobe change, I want her in black lace."

Holly glanced up at Luka with a startled expression.

He shot her a knowing look.

Yes, he'd expressed interest backstage, wanting to see her in black lace. Still, today was not the time, and a music video was definitely not the place. She refused to parade about in black lace, in front of this predominantly male crew. She opened her mouth to protest.

Luka winked at Holly as a devilish grin wrapped around the corners of his mouth and turned his back to her. "Lil, I want her every chaps wicked fantasy."

"Every chap or yours?" Lilly questioned with a cautious edge.

Luka ignored her.

Lilly left muttering, "Fuck! Always last minute changes."

Luka moved in close once more, oh so close.

Holly struggled to do the simple task of breathing to protest her costume again.

Luka interrupted her thoughts and assured her.

"Lil's a pro, ready to fulfill any of my last minute whims. As I will make sure you do ... tonight." His face filled with a sexy expression, promising to make her fly.

Luka's outspoken confidence scorched Holly's pride, placing a blush on her cheeks, she was sure would last a week. She couldn't bring herself to look at Peter because Luka's territorial remark made her want to explain to him, but as usual, Luka's cellular phone buzzed.

Luka turned to answer as Lilly whirled in carrying the latest candidate for Luka's approval. He nodded yes while straightening out the other crisis.

Lilly handed Holly the dress and gave her an 'I only work here' look.

Holly took what there was of the dress and stepped behind a screen. She squeezed her lean body into the tight, black lace fabric. She knew there was no way on Earth she could walk out in front of people in this harlot's dress. The neckline plunged to her waist, with a sheer heart-shaped panel that stretched across her curvaceous breasts. She pondered if it would be worth the humiliation if Luka would smile greedily when he looked at her mountainous cleavage. The sheer black liner that covered her breasts was so thin it drew attention to her hardened nipples. *No, no, a thousand times no!* Not on this side of Hell would Luka convince her to wear this dress.

Holly stood in the dress and could barely take a step. The dress hugged her legs like a Spandex glove and hung mid-calf. What there was of the back, dropped into a V-point, stopping a breath away from the valley of her derrière. The only feature, she liked, was the long, sheer, black sleeves covering her arms to her wrist, accentuating her fresh crimson manicure by Peter's assistant.

Holly opened her mouth to protest as Peter coaxed her into the makeup chair. "I can't wear this!" she declared, her eyes pleading with Luka's reflection in the mirror.

Luka came close to her ear and spoke softly, but it was a command. "You can ... and you will."

This was his cool tone of voice she'd bet he used when he needed to persuade women to do what he wanted. His eyes narrowed, became stormy and pinned her in the mirror.

Holly could feel the tension tightening in her chest choking her. She had to tell him no. *I can't do this, don't make me,* she screamed into the secret place of her mind.

Luka moved closer, and his mouth touched her ear with melting sweetness, which was irresistible. A smooth, persuasive tone of voice followed. "Do this for me. Show them how a classy lady looks."

Luka dropped his warm, powerful hand onto her shoulder, resting it to punctuate his meaning. As if he'd settled the crisis, he massaged her knotted shoulder muscles.

She shut her eyes and felt Luka's electric energy flow into her, bringing her courage while Peter stood in front of her applying makeup.

*Did anyone ever say no to Luka Hunter?*

# Chapter Thirteen

# MAGIC MAN

Holly stared at Luka sporting a boyish grin. She would wear the damn dress! Peter flitted about reacting to the tension in the enclosed space. He applied heavy foundation makeup and a red-hot lipstick to her full lips. He made up her brown doe-eyes with a smoky eyeshadow and applied thick layers of black mascara to the lashes. Three-inch, spiky black, stiletto heels, arrived at Luka's request, to cover her black, silk stocking feet. The shoes made her five-foot-six-inch frame appear sleek, and languid.

Through it all, Luka sat inches away on a stool, watching her. What was locked behind those cool blue magic eyes of his? Was he re-creating Carrin? Whatever he was doing, he was taking her on an adventure, and she loved every minute.

She stared at the unfamiliar reflection in the mirror. Who was this seductress that once resembled conservative Holly Hill that was now heading to perform in a rock video? It seemed Luka knew her better than she knew herself. That unnerved her. Who was this Svengali, this alchemist that coupled with a wave of his hand, transformed her into a stunning beauty?

Holly nervously stepped outside the trailer understanding the apprehension, and excitement a baby bird felt when first pushed from the nest. She heard Luka's sweet voice, his footfall following close behind her.

Luka reached out and gently held her hand as if she was a princess. He escorted her down each step, bathing her in his words of praise. "Now, the entire world will know what a beauty you are."

She saw the pride flash like lightning in his eyes as they widened and sparkled at the sight of her.

"Look at me." She quietly proclaimed under her breath, wanting to shout to the world how beautiful Luka made her feel, made her believe she was.

When they entered the Hard Rock, a man called out to her that he needed to measure the light. Luka led her to the set as Holly stepped over, and around what seemed like hundreds of miles of coiled video cable scattered everywhere. Short, half-circles of railroad tracks, surrounded the set.

Luka pointed, and directed. "Your mark is here. The stage technician will turn on the wind machine to blow the wisps of your hair. I want you to turn slowly toward the camera, so your hair wraps around your face."

He continued to explain the scene. However, the directions, he delivered next, floored her.

"Kaine will step out of the mist and walk up close behind you. I want you to pretend at first, to be unaware of his presence."

*Kaine*!

He'd said, Kaine. Pretend.

*How am I going to be able to pretend to know the world's most beautiful, and sexy man wasn't close by?*

Luka stepped up behind her and she felt his heat radiating as he instructed.

"Here I'll show you."

Holly's knees were melting.

*Kaine! Touch me.*

Luka continued, but she heard little.

*Kaine?*

"Here's the setup. You're in the arms of your lover as the lyrics suggest, 'now that I've found you,' and you want to enjoy him."

*Lover? In the arms of my lover!*

"Relax."

*Relax. How?*

Luka held her from behind for a long moment and then moved around to face her. Shocked by his directions, her face must have reflected her doubts loud, and clear, as she looked into Luka's confident eyes, so blue, so dreamy, and she forced a troubled smile. No one told her the *Hurrikaine* would touch her … intimately.

Again, she wanted to scream, *don't make me do this.*

She frantically searched Luka's eyes that told her she was the only woman in the world that could do this. She calmed her voice and suggested. "I'll pretend I'm in your arms."

"I wouldn't have it any other way. I was rather hoping I would catch that look you have for me on film."

"Is that why?" she quickly demanded with a steady voice.

It all made sense.

"Why what?" His eyebrows arched, and his eyes filled with puzzlement.

"Why you keep me at a distance? Why your eyes always tell me yes? How I excite your body with my touch. But every time, you push me away and say no. Have we been in rehearsal? Are you teaching me to act out how I ache for you? Have you been playing director? You could have asked me, Luka, don't you know, I'd have done anything to please you."

"Trust me. I can't answer all of your questions, but my intentions were sincere. I don't have the time to explain."

As usual, his persuasive blue eyes were hard to fight. Trust him. She didn't know. Had these past hours been a setup? Once again, the nagging insecurities were barely out of snickering distance.

"Stay close." She pleaded with reluctance. "So I can see you."

"Brilliant! I knew I could count on you. Remember, I won't ever be far away from you."

She released a ragged breath.

"Ready?"

Holly nodded yes.

*Could she ever be ready for Kaine?*

"It's S-H-O-W-T-I-M-E!" Luka yelled.

He turned away and let go of her waist only to have his hand magnetically find hers. He squeezed it for encouragement.

She looked up to find the band staring at her with looks of disbelief pasted on their faces. The flush rose quickly to sting her cheeks. She glanced back to Luka whose smile radiated as he watched her.

What was the band witnessing?

Luka picked up a megaphone and shouted out. "Play the track to give Holly, a feel for it." He looked at her, and flashed a bright sunny smile, and encouraged, "You'll be great. Show me how you feel."

He yelled, "Music!"

*Show me how you feel. He'd kept using those words in bed.*

She couldn't think about that anymore.

The loudspeakers blasted the new song, and the sounds were so powerful it pounded the beat into her body with the frightening strength of the stadium concert. Anticipation crept into her psyche as a cat in the night. The haunting and provocative love song displayed a powerhouse guitar track backed with heart-searing lyrics. Evidently, Kaine had written this. The words to the song were making her knees weak picturing how she would lean next to Kaine singing these powerful words. The dance of the elephants in Holly's stomach had twisted into a constant ache, warning her it would not be that easy to get through the first take.

She wanted to stop this foolishness, she wasn't a music video actress, she was part of a distinguished criminal law team. How had this happened? Her fears escalated forcing her to wonder, how much of a fool she about to make of herself.

She glanced over to her gentle, angel-eyed Luka memorizing everything about him, hoping it would be enough to complete the first take, and calm her stomach. The emotionally riveting song ended, and the room went dark. She waited, transfixed in the darkness. Somebody turned on a single, white light, to shine down on her to signal the beginning.

The soundtrack blasted again.

She heard Luka say with a raised voice. "This is a take. Holly, stay on your mark. When the drums crash, the wind machine will turn to you, two measures later, the mist will start, and at the end of the opening vocal line, Kaine will come for you."

Holly tried to move her head to nod yes.

She couldn't move.

She froze as if a deer caught in headlights.

She heard Luka call out loud.

"Ready? Music."

The love song started, and Luka's haunting words echoed in her mind, terrifying her.

*Kaine will come for you.*

# Chapter Fourteen

# CRAZY FOR YOU

H olly stood alone in the center of the Hard Rock Café — waiting. She couldn't see Luka. Her body was trembling. Was it anxiety or pure terror? She was waiting for Kaine, a spectacularly alluring man, an outlaw rock star that had everything.

Luka called out. "Quiet. Action."

Music blasted across the café, spreading a mystical enchantment, like a fairy tale's mist by morning's light. She could barely see Chris' silhouette in the shadows imitating his tight bass line, the sound deep, soft, and muted, careening into a sultry and sexy beat. Somewhere behind her, Michael chimed in on his drums. The jarring sound caused her to jump from her mark. Nicky stood to her right, and the fiery tingle of his lead guitar crested smoothly on the backdrop of Michael's sweet metal tapping. Ian stood out of view to her left. His keystrokes dropped notes like stitches on intricate lace and filled the dimly lit café with a haunting, melodic run that bewitched Holly's fantasies. He was introducing Kaine, the rock superstar — a dangerous, and forbidden man.

From nowhere, calm washed over her as she anticipated Kaine's silky, smooth voice. An addicting voice she'd loved for years. If Kaine were the man she expected, he could persuade her spirit of adventure to perform as she had never dared, never dreamed.

The wind machine blew softly, nipping at her cheeks. She turned her head and saw Luka standing close by in the misty shadows. He sent her an encouraging, sunny smile. *Mmmm,* she would always wish to please Luka.

The beer's fresh buzz and the melodic music completely relaxed her. The powerful song slowly invited her into the seductive melody that quietly called her body to complement the rhythm. She drifted into the melody, swaying like a newly planted sapling bending its branches in a gentle breeze. Her long, reddish-locks blew wispily across her face, bringing a half smile of pleasure with them.

She was falling into the mood of love. Fantastic new feelings fluttered inside her, not of lust, but a peaceful awakening of romance. She gently exhaled and saw the smoky mist rise from behind to circle her feet.

It cautioned ... Kaine was close ... oh, so close. A sensual blend of leather and intoxicating cologne reached the fringe of her senses heralding Kaine's imminent arrival. The voice with no edges followed, surrounding her, engulfing her, and claiming her, promising to seduce her.

Kaine Walker entered her life riding the edge of the wind.

Kaine's scented body heat blew about her with gauzy gentleness, inviting a gush of warm emotions to grow within her. Before she could exhale, his fingertips slid around her waist. His touch brought chills to dance upon her skin as she sank slowly into a quiet submission, positive his fingers were all that kept her from floating away.

She stepped backward into his body, close, closer, so close she lost all sense of where she was as Kaine wove his lyrics of love, wistfully around her sentimental heart. His poetic words summoned her buried feelings of love. Words that demanded she remain brave and allow them to rise to the surface. His lyrics explained how she didn't need to be afraid, for he understood love, the now, and the forever of it.

The back of Holly's head rested softly in the valley of his chest. Her breath quickened with each passing moment. Kaine's tranquil voice pulled her deeper into his mysterious abyss. He promised he wouldn't stop until she was crazy in love with him. She molded her lower back against his hips, he purposefully rubbed against her, straining to slip his knee between her legs, but the restrictive dress would not allow his entry. No matter, she welcomed his sensuality, smothering her senses, closing in on her tighter, and tighter.

"Holly? Holly!" Luka called out, his voice faint. "Listen. Slowly … open your eyes. Look at me … then close them."

Holly struggled to respond to Luka's directions. But, how? She was lost in the whirling depths of an electrifying force. Her eyelids were heavy, drenched in this dream state. Her heart had become hopelessly trapped as if in quicksand, unable to leave the cloistered trance. There was no way she could break Kaine's compelling enchantment — not even for Luka. All, she felt, was Kaine's magnificent body moving with her, fused as one, synchronized to the pounding of the bass and drums.

Luka vanished.

Lost somewhere between the quickening of wild impatience and the alarming masculine scent of Kaine, Holly felt alive. She felt his chest fill with breath, and softly spoke the lyrics of the tempestuous love song into her ear. She smiled and obediently followed Kaine's body as they slowly swayed as one.

"Brilliant! Keep it going." She heard Luka's voice say faintly in the distance.

*Keep it going? As if, she could stop the landfall of the Hurrikaine.*

She fell deeper and deeper into the blinding romance.

Kaine taught her the ways of his seductive dance. He tantalized her skin with the slow movement of his hands until she was breathless. His warm, silky cheek dropped to rest against her neck. His hot tongue touched her skin swiftly, daring her to stop him as his soft lips covered each rapturous inch of her neck. He was close, oh, so close to the shell of her ear when he pleaded in a breathy voice.

"Never ... ever ... leave me...."

*What?* Had she heard him correctly?

*Never leave him. Was he speaking to her, or reciting lyrics?*

Hot and cold shivers ran in contradiction over the flesh of her neck as he placed his searching lips on her neck tenderly retracing the tracks of his tongue.

*Mmmm,* she felt free, so uninhibited and safely locked within the sanctity of his arms. Her body quaked with sensual tremors from the large circles his fingertips traced beneath her belly. The burn was searing as she swayed back and forth lost in a cocoon of fleshly abandon until something unexpected occurred.

Kaine withdrew his hands, and as he moved away, a brittle chill engulfed her.

Holly struggled to be brave, to open her eyes and turn her head to look directly into Kaine's eyes. She needed to see the man that held her captive. But before she opened her eyes, her body spun in a half-circle, followed by a loud crescendo in the music. Twisted and confused, she didn't understand what direction she faced.

Once again, a light mist of scent from Kaine came familiarly close to her face, and she drew in another richly scented breath of his enchanting cologne and aromatic leather garments. His hands masterfully circled her body where they came to rest on her naked back, branding his palm print on her flesh, as he pulled her deeper into the warm, sacred circle within his arms.

She brushed his chest with her breasts.

*Oh, he felt, sooo good, sooo wonderful, sooo sensual, so perfect.*

Incredible as it seemed, she realized she still hadn't laid an eye on this charismatic nomad. But she'd known this bewitching man forever — perhaps in another lifetime — perhaps for many lifetimes. The feel of his sensual body, the tender touch of his hands on her was all too familiar. She knew from her research, he was unbearably gorgeous, but she hadn't understood that he would be so irresistible.

Kaine's heat moved closer. And lost in the awe of him, she instinctively turned her face toward the heat of him. Her fingertips quickly slid up his muscular arms and joined behind his neck, under his hair, as an urgent hunger flared in her movements. And as if he'd read her mind, she felt the delicate touch of his sweet-scented lips brush a light introduction upon hers. His lips felt soft, gentle but carried an immediate eruption of growing passion that started in her head and ended in her heart.

As Kaine continued to press his lips and kiss her, he invited her to begin the dance again with him, to follow his swaying movements, his leg pressing against her. His kiss had developed into an all-consuming pledge that was searing her to him as he kissed her with infinite potency.

Kaine, able to whisk Holly away, far away, to a timeless place she'd never been, and never wanted to leave.

She pushed her hands up into his soft, fragrant hair. She took hold of a full lock, and wove her fingers within, pulling hard, parted her lips, and tilted her head to fit him. For a second she hesitated, waiting for Kaine to enter. He did not disappoint, and as expected, Kaine's warm velvet tongue slipped in with the wave of a deep groan buried in his chest. His kiss was powerful, mysterious, the depth unknown. The sweet kiss took over like a vintage wine warming her from the inside and blossomed with an incredible intensity that promised to consume her.

Meltdown.

Her body went limp with intoxication.

Kaine filled her mouth with his spirited tongue, drinking her in, pumping her mouth as if it were teeming with an eternal fountain of kisses. Kaine tangled his hands in long locks of her hair, pulling her even nearer, threatening to swallow her whole. She felt the tormenting cry in his throat more than she heard it. His body a perfect fit, and drowning in what she would one day hope to call love, she lifted her leg and wrapped it around his.

He pressed his hard bulge against her.

The seduction was complete. She accepted the kiss as Kaine's trademark on her forever. The music faded, but she was sure there had never been a kiss as devoted as theirs was between strangers.

A sudden reserve mixed with rising panic seized Holly. She couldn't give up Kaine, not now. What could she do to stop Kaine from ending the greatest moment of her life? An extraordinary kiss. A perfect kiss, she would treasure the rest of her days. She forced her glazed eyes open.

She struggled for breath as she gazed into the impassioned blue eyes of — Kaine.

# TO BE CONTINUED...

Dear Reader,

Excited to read *TEMPTATION (Part 2)?*

Please take a moment and leave a few comments about your favorite scenes wherever you purchased *HEART.* It is critical to the series to have feedback while the pleasure from the story is fresh in your mind. Thank you for your valuable support.

YOU ROCK!

### A hopeful woman...

Holly Hill did not expect to fall under the fairy tale spell of drop dead gorgeous Luka Hunter.

### A charming man...

Luka Hunter, a rock music executive, has admitted to Holly, there may be a chance at love for them. But will Luka stop Holly from leaving with the womanizing rock star?

### A charismatic man...

Kaine Walker, lead singer for the rock band Hurrikaine, is everything he should be — beautiful, sexy, and forbidden.

What will Holly do...?

### Will she say no?

http://www.kewtownsend.com/

# KEW TOWNSEND

## Affairs of the Heart Series – London

### *HEART* (Part 1)

Forthcoming:
*TEMPTATION* (Part 2), *PROMISES* (Part 3),
*DEVOTED* (Part 4), *BETRAYAL* (Part 5)

Ms. Townsend writes romantic music fiction set in the 1960s-1980s rock scene in *Affairs of the Heart Series*. She lives in sunny Southern California, where she loves to write under a palm tree with the wave's crashing along the shoreline. KEW's love of rock music began at a very young age when she returned glass Coke bottles for change to buy 45 rpm records. Her interested moved from the music to the musicians. Living in Hollywood, she began her journey by interviewed the Beatles when they originally landed at Los Angeles International Airport. Acquiring a taste for the funny Englishmen, she eventually dated one of the Rolling Stones that exposed her to sex, drugs, and rock and roll. Later, her rock star memories surfaced in the *Affairs of the Heart Series* where she weaves her behind the scenes anecdotes with her long love of castles, mysteries, lightning, and thunder into a romantic suspense story. Her master's degree in Cultural Anthropology and Archaeology adds to her world travels, and flavor to her novels.

## CONTACT KEW

### kewtownsend.com

Leave a message, a review, and sign up for the NEWSLETTER. Be first to hear about new releases, preorders, sales, prizes, giveaways, and fun events.